CHAPTER 1

For the end of the world it felt a little mundane. Anticlimactic.

I'd laughed when people said the apocalypse would be brought about by zombies. Ironically, it was the zombies that sustained the rat race. Hoards of the living dead flocked to jobs that, every day, killed a little more of their soul. Worst of all, I was one of them.

No one else noticed the end was not only nigh but had actually been and gone. People carried on as before. Pretending life still had some kind of meaning and purpose. The reality that we all just hurtled around on a clump of rock heading directly for the sun had little impact on my fellow commuters.

"Hold the door." A disembodied voice called from behind.

I looked up briefly from my phone reluctant to make contact with another so called human.

Still no horsemen of the apocalypse. No rivers of fire or blood; or whatever it was that was supposed to harken the end of existence. The world had ended and yet, everything was much the same.

Perhaps, it was only my little world that had ended.

I paused briefly, reluctant to enter through the gateway of Hell (or RM Smith's Financial Consultancy as it's known to the fellow hostages). I still had to make the conscious effort to walk through the door. Even after all these months daily attendance had not become habit. That number one bestselling book was wrong. I should have taken it back and demanded a refund. There were so many things I should have done.

"Are you going in?" Impatience in his tone this time.

I shouldn't have asked someone else to hang around and observe this bizarre little ritual. Only, I hadn't asked him. He was just inconveniently there.

The old dude glanced at his watch. Twelve minutes late for work. That's practically early.

"Employees aren't supposed to use this door." His disgruntled voice snipped.

Of course, my first interaction of the day was negative. That was how the world worked now.

Just keep looking at the phone, Jen. Don't make eye contact.

"Did you hear me?" The agent of the machine wouldn't be ignored.

I admired him a bit for that. The moment we entered this building we'd all be ignored. Maybe, on some level, cease to exist. The induction video had said, 'we are all

"I loved it!"

(My Mum)

"Do you have a spare copy? I spilt tea on this one."

(My Best Friend)

"What's that you're writing?"

(My Nephew)

FOR MUM

MY OWN LITTLE PERSONAL ARMAGHEDDON

WRITTEN BY

GILLIAN LEE GIBSON

part of something bigger' but, much like a cult, it never articulated what that was.

"Hello?" He added, impatiently.

Alright! Who are you, my Dad? You get paid as much to do a good job as you do to do a half assed one; and I was master of the half assed.

"Well, if you don't step aside, I'm not going to be an employee. The mad old bint who owns this place is doing one of his 'walk rounds'. Care in the community more like. If I'm not there to make his coffee, well, I suppose someone else will. Then they'll all tipple to the fact that I am completely surplus to requirements and I can't go back to the Job Centre. They hate me there."

Neil, my personal advisor, had been off for six weeks with stress. I'd been name checked in his doctor's note.

"Is this what your generation calls oversharing?" He had what I would call a 'historical-drama-English-accent'.

For a second, I was almost interested. Some poor sucker had fallen on harder times than me.

Maybe he'd say , 'just doin' it for the lols' to brighten my day. I could do with a laugh.

No, today would be different. According to that article I could make that choice here and now. I just had to focus on the present. The article was called something like, 'Finding the past unbearable?' It was little surprise it was bigging up the now. It could have been an advert. I didn't get to read to the end. The shopkeeper pulled the old, 'are you going to buy that? This isn't a bloody library,' routine. The newsagents was indeed different in one respect. Creepy Chris wasn't hanging around the human biology session exposing himself. Well, not on a Monday at least. He had to sign on.

"Oversharing would be if I brought up menstrual cramps. Or the drought of male admirers since my ex ghosted me."

Where the heck did 'menstrual cramps' come from? Maybe this is the much awaited mental breakdown. My parents would be relieved. 'Well, she's finally snapped, Johnny. Here she is dressed as a panda.'

'Naw, love,' Dad would say, because somehow in my head my parents are from Runcorn. 'That's just the onesie your sister Jeanie bought her for Christmas."

Ah well, they say a change is as good as a rest.

"Oh, I am sorry." The English Regent sounded almost compassionate." Did your boyfriend die?"

Sure, ignore my womanly pain. "Chance would be a fine thing."

"I can't see why they would hate you at the Job Centre." The compassionate tone replaced by familiar exasperation.

Great, 9:15 and I'd already made another fan. Hang on, did I start at nine or quarter too?

"They said I had a terrible attitude." I wasn't exactly Chumba wumbaing (getting knocked down and getting up again); at least I wasn't managing to do it with a smile on my face. I'd had a terrible, cataclysmic, life changing event that I had to try constantly not to think about.

10

It didn't work.

No, stop. Breathe. Focus on the positive. At least I had a job.

The curse of 'at least'. The sentence starter I had come to dread. 'At least you found out before things got serious'. We had been in relationship for seven years. We had lived together for five. How much more serious could things have been?

'At least' and all the platitudes that followed were a verbal tic. Space for the orator to take a mental breath. A play for time to scrabble for hope amongst the ruins and desperation of my life. The conclusion was all but apparent; 'no survivors here.'

I had zero tolerance for inane conversation. Particularly before morning coffee. That little treat had been the first to go in the new round of budget cuts from my 'debt management councillor'. Or, as I preferred to think of him, the 'fun tax inspector.' His sacred task, handed down through the generations, was to destroy any semblance of a life I might have left post 'event.' The article said I should choose a fun euphemism to talk about the bad thing that happened and minimise its impact. Hence, 'the apocalypse'. The fun inspector didn't like that either but, he didn't like much. He thought referring to the event as an 'apocalypse' may be 'perpetuating the negative thought pattern that prolongs the impact on life outcomes'. I mean, I'd had to move back in with my parents and all my bank accounts were frozen, but apparently, it's all in how I talk about it.

I found the courage to unceremoniously barge past the self-appointed doorman. A better employee would have asked who he was to use the side door, or as I called it, 'the secret overtime accumulator', but I was fresh out of breezy conversation.

"Oh," I turned back to rescue the situation. I remembered my probationary period and what my mentor/babysitter kept subtly referencing as my 'off putting personality and interactive style'.

"That's another minor Royal having a baby." I held up my phone to show him the social media article. I half expected to be burnt as a witch for capturing images of people in my magic device. Still, I believe this is what may be termed 'water cooler conversation'.

"Babies having babies." There. That was friendlier. I could feel a bit less guilty about thinking, hopefully not saying, that he was a waste of space.

Neil (pre-breakdown) highlighted it was 'hard to tell what just falls out of your head and into your mouth and what you consciously choose to say'. Still, I can't have been the only reason he was crying that day. I mean, he works in the Job Centre. It doesn't quite say, 'abandon hope all ye who enter' above the door, but it's heavily implied.

CHAPTER 2

"Afternoon Jen." David looked pointedly at his watch.

David was the worst kind of management; middle management. The completely unnecessary layer of the organisation Dave buzzed around the office looking all important. We had to pretend we thought he was important and that his job definitely couldn't have been done by a monkey in a suit. Come to think of it the monkey probably didn't even need a suit. The Job Centre was full of 'Dave's' and there were an abundance of jobs for them. Nothing that could give life meaning but, fortunately, nothing that required any real training or skill.

Me on the other hand. Well, I was so far down the pecking order people actually thought I was important. All the other assistants were well organised and super efficient. I'd successfully managed to buck that trend for three months. I achieved the dream of mostly blending into the background. People had learnt I wasn't worth their time. Occasionally, I was asked to make coffee but only when there was literally no one else.

"It's still morning." It would be morning for the next three years. At least, that was how it would feel. Time passed differently within these walls.

"Cognitive functioning is the first to go at your age, Dave." I mocked compassion.

I knew David hated having his name abbreviated only slightly less than he hated me. I don't know why he didn't just fire me. I couldn't quit. Neil had been clear about that.

"Can you tell me who the Prime Minister is?" I raised my voice and spoke very slowly.

"Can you?" He sneered.

Nope, but I can name three generations of the Kardashians.

"This is the last time I cover for you." Dave stomped back into his office.

It wouldn't be. He'd said the same thing last week, before the photocopier incident. Who knew it could also scan documents and email them to everyone? I'd learnt a hard lesson. Next time I would just pinch the magazine from the break room, or rip out the relevant pages. Still, I consider my contribution to the working environment a rather informative update to all staff on breast augmentation.

"Sorry Dave." I called after him. "I have really bad cramps."

His office door slammed closed.

My 'desk buddy', Janice, glared. I'd betrayed the sisterhood again. What Janice didn't realise was wee Dave was now in his office plucking up the courage to point out I must have the longest cycle on the planet; women's troubles was my go to excuse. Janice also failed to understand that if it wasn't for the patriarchy, she or I could be sitting behind that imposing mahogany desk. Well, Janice could. I had no idea (or interest) in what this company actually did. Having Janice as my 'desk buddy' was the equivalent to a school being put on 'special measures'. I must have had the longest induction period in history.

"I meant to ask him if we were still on for work tomorrow." I stared at the firmly closed door.

"We are *on* for work every day. Eight thirty to five PM."

I was way off in both the start and finish time. It seemed unlikely I would have agreed to that.

As if you had a choice.

"You have to stop texting him that first thing in the morning too. Some of us are busy!" Janice snapped.

I hated Janice with a passion that burned brighter than the fire of a thousand suns. Janice was a chameleon. I'd watched her take an interest in mediation, mindfulness and hot yoga as the trends came and went. Janice smacked of a middle aged, dissatisfied housewife in the throes of a midlife crisis. Janice was constantly on the lookout for the next quick fix to fill the void of her existence. Only Janice wasn't married, or much older than me; maybe. It was hard to tell under all that make-up.

Janice had chosen a gentle middle of the road life. Like the newest man in her life Janice had a good job (I think. It seemed better paid than mine). This new man had 'stable prospects' (whatever that meant). FYI apparently not that he looks like a horse or has any enviable horse anatomy.

"How's the new bloke, Janice?"

Another scowl. That was not the face of a woman with a boyfriend hung like a horse.

"We're in love." Her voice lacked conviction.

I couldn't help thinking Janice loved what's-his-face because she'd chosen to. Geoff (it seemed likely to be something like Geoff but with a weird pronunciation like Ge-oe-ff) . Ge-oe-ff was 'a safe pair of hands'. There would be no surprises with him. Janice wouldn't wake up one morning to find he'd skedaddled with all her money and most of her future. I envied Janice. No I didn't. I hated her. I was getting confused.

Janice tapped a pile of papers on my desk. They'd been there for about a week. I was supposed to have done something with them. I just wasn't sure what. It was pretty impressive that in twelve weeks I was no further forward in identifying what the company did and, within that, what my role was. When anyone asked I said, 'finance'. People would nod knowingly; because honestly that's so boring, to elaborate further would have stopped time. There were never any follow up questions. It now felt like a daily challenge not to learn anything new. My Bluetooth headphones had been a boon. I'd listened to several audio books and even considered learning French.

I heard on the grapevine (social media) that Neil is on a phased return back to work. He'd be pleased to know I was still in the same dead end job he'd assigned before he ran from his office, weeping. I still don't know how his tie was on fire.

Janice looked at the papers again. This time she raised an eyebrow. Well, some sort of caterpillar she'd trained to sit where her eyebrow used to be. It was comical when Janice tried to move her face under all that foundation. I was fairly confident she had on three sets of false eyelashes. They kept clumping together and she'd screw her face (she thought discretely) to separate them. It was bloody hilarious.

"You alright, Janice? You look like you're having a stoke."

More death stares as Janice looked at the pile of papers again.

I nodded knowingly. Well, I think it was knowingly. I might just have looked as though I had wind. I'd wait until Janice was otherwise distracted (work or a shiny surface - either could hold her attention) then I'd stick them all in the shredder. Problem solved. Ha, and Neil said I didn't have leadership skills. Ok, he said I didn't have the qualifications to head up BUPA but I told him I was a bit of a hypochondriac and willing to learn (sort of).

"Coffee." Dave stuck his head out of his office door.

I resisted the urge to say, 'thanks' and pretend I thought he was the one making it. I quite liked Dave, in a way. It was a shame I was going to have to report him to HR when he eventually plucked up the courage to ask about my monthlies. So, I repressed the urge to point out Janice was never asked to make coffee. I suppose because she understood her job, and appeared to be pretty efficient at getting it done. Janice never spilled nail varnish over the monthly reports. Lovely in the black Janice had money for her nails to be professionally tended. She didn't...

Stop, don't think about it. The magazine article said don't let yourself think about the bad thing that happened. Think about something nice.

Ha! It was funny when Neil tripped over the cat that followed me into the Job Centre. Ok, so maybe I had encouraged it in with a tuna sandwich. Anyone could see Neil was stressed and a bit lonely since his girlfriend left him for, what I am to understand, was her own cousin. I thought the cat could be like a therapy pet. How I to know Neil was allergic? Or that the cat had mange?

CHAPTER 3

"Hello again." The nuisance from the door interrupted as I boiled the kettle in the kitchen. He smiled warmly as though we were chums.

We weren't.

I tried to avoid eye contact but he lowered his eyes to meet mine. My stomach churned. That would be karma. Mocking women's troubles only to become afflicted. Thankfully, it was more of a flutter than a mind numbing pain. I didn't want to kill anyone either. Well, no more so than usual. Probably just the 'breakfast burrito' Mum had micro-waved earlier. I suspected, even as I ate it, I'd be seeing that again.

"We met at the door." He smiled again.

I didn't. You can't encourage these people. One weak moment and suddenly you're on the social committee, in charge of the tea fund or having to go harass people to contribute to Susan's baby fund; and no one likes Susan. I'd tried to get involved in the office baby shower but apparently running a book on who the father might be wasn't 'in the spirit' of the event'. If you asked me (and apparently no one did) Susan would have appreciated some narrowing of the odds.

I looked up from my coffee making antics and gave a nod of pretend recognition. I felt my breath catch as my eyes met his. Great, all that was going on in life and now I was getting sudden onset asthma.

This was the kind of man my Mum would have called distinguished. The historical-drama-English-accent matched the vision before me. Pin striped suit, slightly greying hair. A bit of a 'silver fox'.

Could I be one of those women turned on by power? Or the allure of finance?

I smiled.

No! No smiling.

"You were auditioning for a part in the zombie apocalypse." He pulled out his phone and mimicked being oblivious to the rest of the world.

"Who told you about the zombie apocalypse?" The air flew again from my lungs. The world started again to wobble on its axis.

"No one had to tell me." He quipped. "I see the zombies everywhere."

"Is that supposed to be funny?"

Stop, Jen. I fought against the tears. He doesn't know. He can't possibly know.

"You were engrossed in your phone." His voice confused. Aware he'd somehow caused massive offence.

20

"Why did you say that?" My voice cracked.

You know why he said it, Jen.

"I held the door." He tried to reset out interaction. "There aren't really zombies." His tone so genuinely sincere I almost warmed to him.

I was almost relieved too; until I realised the prize for his ignorance was that I got to stay here.

"You're not supposed to hold the door open for people. It's a security risk." I pushed my way to the coffee. I had shown vulnerability. I had to pull it back.

"I could have been a terrorist."

"This coffee is the act of terror." He sniffed the offending liquid in his mug.

I thought of the cinnamon lattes that used to start my day. "It is. I switched the coffee for toner last month."

"Is that a joke? That stuff's highly toxic."

I shrugged. "I don't drink it."

He sniffed his mug again. This time more cautiously.

I was rapidly losing interest. This man made me uncomfortable. I would have said exposed but I'd already thought about Creepy Chris today and was fairly confident after last Thursday's 'incident' I had some kind of post traumatic stress. It's a sad reflection of my life that having a penis placed on top of your handbag doesn't even make it into the top ten of challenges in a week.

"You're new here. How are you finding the place?" He tried again to make conversation. He had his coffee.

There were loads of other places to waste time. Loads of other people to do it with too.

"Google maps at first. I know the way now."

One bus. That was one of the biggest attractions. That and I heard the building had a gym. It didn't.

I'd been here three months. Twelve weeks. Five days a week. Seven hours a day. Four hundred and twenty hours of my life. Well, give or take. I come and go as I please; it's part of my charm.

"Are you enjoying the job?"

He seemed unperturbed by my RBF. It was my own mother who first told me that I had it. Only, she thought it meant 'really bright future' rather than 'resting bitch face'. Cousin Carol snorted and said, 'I think you got it right first time'.

I wanted to quip that I wasn't aware I was here for my own entertainment. This job was payback, retribution... *No, think happy thoughts*. Choose to be positive. The article said to replace a sad memory with a happy one. At least one day I'd be dead.

Wow! I was rubbish at this 'self-help' crap. I wished I could afford a proper therapist. I should ask Dave if therapy is one of the 'perks' of working here. He bangs on a lot about prestige. Not actual tangible rewards.

Oh, the silver fox was still waiting for an answer.

"I might enjoy the job. If I ever find out what it is I'm supposed to be doing. This place is like a level of Dante's Hell. Every day much like the last." That was one of those 'brutally honest' moments when Neil said it would be better just to say, 'fine'.

"It's fine." I remembered the smile. I think I scared him. "I'd better get back to whatever it is I'm supposed to be doing."

"The mad old bint not made an appearance on your floor yet?" He looked at me meaningfully. As though we were in on some kind of joke.

We weren't.

"It would be hard to say. This place is full of the walking dead." I pretended to be a zombie then stopped. Zombies ruined my life.

He laughed and for a second and in spite of myself, I liked him. He was attractive for an older guy. I could say that because I did so as a fully paid up member of the Spinster Society. Just realised that abbreviates to SS. I'll have to think of another name for my organisation. That one could give the wrong impression. Also, 'spinster' has such negative connotations. Maybe I could say I've chosen to live 'man free'. Yes, much better.

"Ron." He held out his hand for me to shake. He'd noticed the shift in my icy demeanour.

"Run where?" I pretended not to have heard his name. People were forgetting mine all the time. Who'd have thought that along with everything else I'd lose my identity too?

"Jen." Odd, I usually give a series of ever more amusing pseudonyms. *Fflangè* was my personal favourite. I used to do an accent until HR pointed out it could be 'wildly misconstrued'. Ron must have caught me unaware.

"What department do you work in, Jen?"

Crap! I didn't even know that.

"I work with David." Everyone knew Dave. "I'm his boss." I declared. Much to my own surprise.

"His boss?" It occurred to me that Ron might know I was lying. "Is he a good employee?"

"He is when he's sober." I laughed. "He will be under my supervision." I tried to sound more professional as I moved towards the door. I didn't know why I was still entertaining this guy.

"I might put him on performance management. He has a very poor attitude."

"Does he?" Ron looked amused.

I had to shut this down, quickly. I wasn't going to get comfortable here. I didn't want to make friends. This wasn't my world. I tolerated Smiths because I'd never belong. There's was a tiny bit of light in my soul that didn't want to just lie back and accept my fate. Maybe that light would burn brighter over the coming months. Maybe it would be extinguished too. For now it gave me some hope that it was there.

"You look familiar." Ron ventured.

"Yeah, from the door. We covered this." I picked up the coffee mugs. "We're running short on milk. I might have to use the correction fluid again."

This time he ignored the bait.

"You'll recognise me from all the trade magazines. They're always doing articles on my success."

Why was I still talking? At some point Ron could ask what it is I do. I'd seen 'mergers and acquisitions' on a door somewhere. Perhaps this version of Jen could do that?

"Did you work in a shop in town?"

I could feel my heart beat louder in my chest. It was almost a relief to know I was still alive. Unless this was a heart attack caused by all the stress. Then the relief would be fairly short lived.

Maybe he'd give you mouth to mouth.

STOP IT!

Mum would have said that was just an 'intrusive thought' and everyone has them; we just don't say them out loud. Intrusive thoughts were the only ones I had. How many intrusive thoughts a day is considered normal? You can't ask people that, can you? They would think I was some kind of weirdo if I asked, 'how many times do you think about trying to pet a fish?' FYI yesterday alone it was seven. All these internal distractions stop me from doing important stuff - like making the tea.

"I was on Crimewatch last week. That'll be it." Too close to the truth.

"I'm pretty good with faces." Ron persisted.

I wondered if he would shut up if I told him I did porn on the side.

"It was the shop on Crawford Street. An antique Bookshop that sold records and..."

I could smell the place. I could feel it. If I closed my eyes I could almost be back there. Six whole months had passed and the pain of the loss was greater than ever. That shop had been my little place in the world. A place I knew and understood. A life according to plan.

I couldn't think about it. Not now. Not ever. I had to pretend that it didn't matter until, one day, I could feel that too. That's what the article said.

"A Bookshop?" I laughed bitterly. "You must think I'm some kind of geek."

CHAPTER 4

I'd managed to pass a good half hour on social media. There was much speculation on the gender of the new Royal baby; they definitely meant assigned sex at birth. I had wanted to comment that but Dave's life was so interminably dull he'd taken to stalking me. He'd notice the time stamp on the post and that would be another 'little chat'. So, instead, I demonstrated good self-regulation, as Neil had always encouraged, and resisted commenting, 'let's just hope it's human. Lol.'

I should start keeping a list of things for Neil to be proud of. I had offered to keep in touch during his absence from work but apparently, 'that wouldn't be helpful'. Neil was 'adjusting to life being single'. Often, when I think how hard I've got it I remember Neil's ex is due a baby with her cousin this month. I wondered if it would be born with fur. Maybe even a tail.

I took comfort knowing Neil would appreciate I'd taken his advice. Sort of. I hadn't sworn at anyone in weeks. Well, not so they could hear anyway.

Neil was always reticent about my use of social media. In my last job I had intended to text my best friend Kate about the budget cuts but accidentally tagged her in a public post. That's how fourteen people found out they were unemployed. Fifteen if you include my unceremonious dismissal. That little 'training need' led me to RM Smiths doing...whatever it is I am supposed to be doing.

"Are you finished?" Janice tapped her false, professionally manicured nails against her desk and looked pointedly at Dave. Janice was eager Dave knew she was a good mentor. I was just a terrible student.

I hadn't understood what she'd asked me to do (something about a spreadsheet formula) and had quickly forgotten there was even a task. I thought it was just a 'keep 'em busy' activity. The kind the teacher gives when hungover; which was pretty often in my school. It was not a good place. Maybe that's why I'd failed in life. I should sue.

"We have a legal department, right?"

It was impressive that despite the layers of foundation the colour could still drain from Janice's face.

"What have you done now?"

People always expected the worst.

"Smith is going to be around soon." Dave looked at his watch. I'd never seen it up close. I hoped it had a Mickey Mouse face and his gloved hands pointed to the appropriate time. "He's apparently on the fourth floor."

Lucky fourth floor.

"Did they go with tracking the elderly? It was fairly controversial but, at least you know where they are when they get all confused and wander off."

Dave glared at me. "When he comes I want you to go and photocopy this." He slammed a pile of papers down on my desk.

"What about this spreadsheet?" I feigned exasperation. As though I was fully committed to the task. As though I understood what the task had been.

Janice nailed the overworked exasperation with a sigh or an almost roll of her eyes (probably as much movement she could muster under the weight of all those false eyelashes). Whenever someone tried to give Janice a task she always seemed busy. Janice had our mentorship the wrong way round. She had much to learn from me; firstly, you had to stop being competent.

"Is this really necessary?" These were copies of *last* month's reports and half way through the pile was a copy of the 'Boob jobs from Hell' article. It wasn't as classy as I had first made it seem.

Janice pulled out a mirror from her desk and began frantically applying makeup. It was difficult to comprehend she had thought to add more. Janice had really nailed that Bride of Chucky look this morning. I'd left last month's *Cosmo* on her desk open at the article, 'Less is more' but she hadn't taken the friendly hint.

Janice glanced at me. Not her usual sharp, 'you're a waste of time and air' look but the vulnerable one. The one you'd catch a glimpse of when she thought no one was looking.

"That colour brings out your eyes." I mean, it didn't. It was in fact three colours of shadow and the kind of fading I'd only seen in comedy but I wanted to say something nice.

I must be nicer to Janice. I know she's scowling at me. I can see the foundation cracking above her 'high def' eyebrows. If I get her in the secret Santa I'll buy her a small trowel so she can more efficiently layer on all that make-up. Bloody Hell, Jen. That's a dreadful thought. You might still be here at Christmas.

My mobile phone buzzed into action.

"Put that away." David barked.

The bank's number lit up on the screen. I threw the mobile phone in the drawer with pleasure. They called with increasing regularity to provide a 'helpful update' that was neither helpful or an update; nothing has changed today either, you're still up the creek. PS we're going to prove you're in on it.

"Who keeps calling you anyway?" There was an edge to Janice's tone.

"I'm a very popular person and, I have a stalker." I tried to make the last part sound intriguing. "In fact, I have two." One was the Detective in charge of the investigation, and the other was Clint the Bank manager. FYI I never refer to him as Clint in my head but, I can't say what I do call him. My parents raised a lady. Well, they tried to.

"When Mr. Smith gets here." Janice appeared lost for words of wisdom. "Just try not to say anything." She was increasingly frustrated by my presence. Janice didn't have Neil's patience. I wonder if I was discussed in the weekly business meeting here too.

I knew people hated me here. I wasn't completely lacking in self-awareness. I hated being here and I couldn't hide it. It was all I could do to drag myself out of bed in the morning since 'the event'. I'd initially been more optimistic. It was all just a big misunderstanding. There would be a rational explanation. Stephen would be back soon and he'd explain calmly what had happened. He'd be overjoyed to know I never doubted him. But the days turned into weeks, the weeks into months and no one had heard from him. The money was gone. Stephen was gone. Eventually the hope was gone too.

"Mr. Smith." David sounded forcefully bright. He looked at the papers on my desk, meaningfully.

I briefly revolted, pushing the breast article further out of the pile.

Dave gave me a thunderous look. It could have stopped time; even on that wee Mickey Mouse watch he was wearing.

David and Janice exchanged looks but never admonished me in front of real people. It would have reflected badly on them. Either that or they wanted others to see just how much they had to endure. Whatever their reasoning, public humiliation wasn't a tactic used to try and keep me in line. I sometimes wondered if the Job Centre paid them to have me here. It was probably a condition of Neil's return to work that I never darkened their door again.

I stood up, daring to catch a glimpse of the octogenarian whose presence had all but shut this place down for the past week.

Oh crap!

CHAPTER 5

"This is Jennifer Blake." David tried to breeze past my existence. Ordinarily, I would have been relieved. Apart from the odd request for coffee, I'd be free to while away my existence as I pleased.

"She's the office junior."

That's not what I told people. I was thirty four for goodness sake. Well, twenty seven according to my application but, even that's old for a 'junior'.

"The Office Junior." Ron repeated in a neutral tone. "So, you're her line manager, David?"

"Yes, but..." Dave trailed off. He wanted to denounce responsibility. Dave had been asked that question many times and it had never yet come with positive feedback.

"Jen was just about to go and do some photocopying." Dave pushed the papers towards me.

"Really." The silver fox smiled. "I thought there was an issue with the toner. Wasn't it running low?"

Dave looked devastated. He loved that photocopier. That's what happens when you stick at these mindless jobs long enough. You become overly attached to office equipment.

I leaned into Janice. "What's it called when people marry objects? Remember that woman who married the Eiffel tower? That'll be Dave with the photocopier."

Janice looked horrified but there was no way that Ron had heard it.

"Ronald Smith." Ron held out his hand. "Pleased to meet you, Jennifer, was it?" He smiled, knowingly, dispelling any hope that he had early onset dementia. Maybe he'll think *I'm* part of some community care project.

RM Smith. I hoped the M was for MacDonald and tried to picture Ron dressed as a clown. Neil said that was a strategy he used to strip people of their power. I bloody hated clowns. Still, it would be more light-hearted and whimsical when Ron eventually fired me.

"Unless you would like a coffee." Dave looked even more hesitant. I was not capable of even making coffee for someone so senior. Senior in the organisation. That wasn't another dig about his age. You have to be clear. Otherwise, it's another sit down with HR.

"No, thank you." Ron was quick, too quick to answer. I resisted the urge to smirk, or tried too. He had a glint in his eye.

No. Stop it. You don't like him. You don't like anyone here.

Janice harrumphed. Acknowledging my existence was a waste of the boss' time.

34

Janice and Dave seemed amazed when I eventually turned up each morning. My commitment to this place was so low they expected one day I just wouldn't come back. To be honest, I was surprised I'd lasted this long.

Janice looked at me impatiently. She had several thousand ideas about how this place could be improved that she was desperate to discuss with Ron. I only had one; and that involved a shed load of petrol and box of matches.

"You remember Janice." Dave smiled as he showed off his prize heifer.

Ron glanced at Janice. I'd spent the past few months blending into the background, not just here, in life. This man had known the old me. The me that wasn't hollowed out inside. The version of me even I had liked.

"As a newcomer Ms. Blake do you have any helpful suggestions on how we can improve?" Ron turned his attention back to me.

I was in for it now.

'Yes, maybe we could explain to newcomers what they should be doing'.

'Perhaps all employees should be encouraged to follow Janice's whimsical sense of fashion and come to work dressed as a clown'.

"I've had a number already." Ron pretended to recall conversations. "From increased security to better coffee."

He was enjoying this!

I hate him! I hate all men without exception. Men are evil and they wreck your life.

Ok, not my Dad, but all other men.

Ok, Neil was alright too. I mean he looked like the living dead when he caught mange from that cat but it scabbed over nicely before he was even signed off.

All other men were evil. You can kiss as many frogs as you like but all you'll ever get are warts. I blame Disney. Brainwashing us. Convincing us Prince Charming was just waiting in the wings to sort out our lives. Bloody woodland creatures don't clean your home either. I'm sure I'd read recently that Disney was a Nazi sympathiser who'd had his head cryogenically frozen to be reanimated when they find a cure for old age (or whatever he died of - being a fascist, maybe). All things given I can't see why I'm surprised Disney lied to children.

Janice looked crestfallen. She slumped behind her desk. This was supposed to have been her chance. She'd been banging on about having 'face time' with Ron for weeks. Full disclosure, I thought Ron was one of her online dating rescues.

Janice wanted to be here, depressing as that might be, she loved this place. This wasn't right. I was having her moment. I should have been jubilant. The new me was supposed to be hard. Screw people over first before they had the chance. That's the winner's way.

That's the dickhead's way.

I don't even like Janice.

Bloody hell...

"I'm just the Office Junior." There. I had admitted it out loud. I had taken some of the power of those words away.

"No one is just anything." Ron corrected. He spoke as though I really mattered. For a second his words brought me silence. It was as if time stopped. As if all the noise in my head stopped too.

"All the same." I smiled. An actual, real life smile. "The person you really want to speak to about making some positive change is Janice."

We'd be hearing about this for months.

Janice looked utterly bewildered. She froze. More so that the usual make-up paralysis.

"You should probably try and schedule a meeting together. Janice could pick her top three changes."

Why was I helping? Stop helping.

Janice continued to stare at me blankly. Maybe she'd finally turned to plastic under all those chemical layers. To think I was worried about zombies.

"You were thinking about the HR online system last week, Janice. Modifications that would reduce the time each employee would have to spend dealing with administrative tasks. I liked that one."

I hadn't really been listening but it was enough to prompt her into an enthusiastic description that enabled me to make a sharp exit.

It was probably just paranoia but I felt the intensity of Ron's gaze as he watched me leave. It made me uneasy to know that after all these months I might finally have been seen.

CHAPTER 6

I was definitely going to get fired this time. Still, I'd had a good run. I would have spent the remainder of the afternoon clearing out my desk if I'd bothered to amass anything other than biscuit wrappers in it.

It was almost inspiring to watch Janice speak with such passion. I assumed no one really knew what they were doing and hence were completely unaware whether colleagues (i.e. me) were doing what they should. Only, Janice would have known, or bothered to have found out, who the mystery man in the kitchen was before she started running her mouth off.

This isn't *all* my fault. He could have said. 'Call me Ron' should have piped up when I was telling him how crappy his organisation was. Although Janice seemed to be telling him the same thing and he really listened. I suppose because she was thinking of how to improve; in a way that didn't involve arson and everyone else turning a blind eye.

I sat down on the bench outside The Bakehouse. It had been a tough day. I deserved a treat. I no longer actually had the money to go in and buy something but I could enjoy the smell for free and, added bonus, no calories. Not that I had to worry about calories. The stress and anxiety of the past few months had done a real turn on my waist. The crippling debt played its part too. Even the budget bakery would have been a stretch. My clothes hung off my skeletal frame. Not even they wanted to be seen with me. I didn't look attractive. At least, I didn't feel it.

I'd be even more screwed without this crappy job.

Breathe. Don't think about it. If he was going to sack you he would have done it there and then. It would have been the ultimate demonstration of dominance to have dismissed you on the spot. He chose not to. Probably something far more humiliating up his sleeve. *No, what did the magazine say?* Think positively. Live in the moment. Right now, you have the smell of baked goods to enjoy. Just breathe. That's free. It's also, 'taking pleasure in the little things'. I am winning at this new positive attitude. I might email Neil and let him know.

"Are you following me?"

The silence and positivity was broken.

"Mr. Smith." I recognised his voice. Maybe he and the others back at the office could be convinced into that social media trend where you looked away and everyone takes a turn to say your name. If you guess each person correctly perhaps he could offer additional days of paid leave.

"Ron." he smiled and sat down next to me on the bench. "Mr. Smith was my father."

"Mr. Smith was a lot of people's father."

"It's a common name." He agreed.

I felt relieved he didn't assume I was implying his Dad put it about (which was exactly what I had been implying).

"You were very kind to Janice earlier." The same expression. Like he was looking at the Times cryptic crossword and not another person.

Kind was not something I considered that I had ever been to Janice. I had merely shifted Ron's focus. It didn't matter to me that Janice looked hurt or upset. It didn't matter to me that Janice cared about meeting Ron. Or that she had been looking forward to it all week. Janice wasn't my friend. I didn't even like her. I wasn't going to care about her. I wasn't going to care about any of them. Dave and Janice were just people I was forced to be in close proximity with. Any warmth of feeling I developed towards them was just some form of Stockholm Syndrome.

"I'm on my lunch." My tone defensive. I had in fact been thirty minutes late this morning and, in my lunch 'hour', I'd already had a ninety minute wander around the shops.

Ron held up his hands in mock surrender. "I'm not checking up on you."

Of course not. I'm far too low down the food chain for that. They probably had a Jen on every floor. Someone who can just drop everything to make coffee for the important people or do some menial photocopying. Mum always tried to cheer me up by telling me that I was the 'office eye candy'. It was more of a depressing reflection on how little feminism had progressed. It was a sobering thought as I passed each day so mundanely my ovaries were literally shrivelling and life was passing me by.

"If I had known who you were." I tried to harness a defence. Neil would be devastated if I was sacked again. It would put his recovery back months.

"You would have been as star struck as the rest of them? I can't imagine it somehow, Jen." Again with the twinkle in his eye.

That could be a serious medical condition. Glaucoma, maybe. Or, maybe he was thinking about how to nick my purse. Ha! Nothing in that but a note from my Mum. 'I still think you're great' with a picture of what I'm fairly confident was supposed to be Tony the Tiger (who I'd apparently loved as child). The drawing looked more like a cry for help.

"Jen." Ron began cautiously.

I liked how he said my name. As though it meant something. Not all exasperated like the others but, with a sense of camaraderie. Maybe Ron hated being at Smiths too. Of course, he got paid a lot more than me to hate it, but I'd long ago accepted life wasn't fair.

Ron looked more serious. Here it comes. The old 'don't bother coming back after lunch' routine, which I had embarrassingly thought on one occasion was just a half day.

"I was right about the shop, wasn't I?"

"Maybe." I looked away. He won't see me cry. No man was ever going to see my cry again. Except again maybe my Dad and that ship had long since sailed with Neil.

"How did you know about the book?" The words came out as a whisper.

"What book?" Ron looked confused.

"The zombie apocalypse?" It was absurd. I hated saying it out loud. My life reduced to this.

"There's a book about a zombie apocalypse?"

"My partner was writing one." Stephen hadn't told many people the 'plot' of what he was sure would be a best seller. He claimed to be too afraid someone would pinch the idea. They'd certainly churn out that twaddle a lot quicker. For Stephen, 'writing a book' seemed to involve a lot of sitting around in his underpants eating cake. The little he had produced was worse than Mum's erratic etching of Tony the Tiger. Although, it probably took about the same time to complete. Stephen thought every word he'd written was gold.

'It's the film rights and merchandise that'll bring in the real money'.

I hadn't wanted to ask. A particular low point was the 'Aberzombie' t-shirt line. He later added 'finch' because it was important to the 'plot' (plot? I'd read it twice and still not a clue). Apparently, it was integral to the story that finches survived. It was certainly integral to what he assumed would be a million dollar marketing deal. Everything was a quick fix with Stephen; even our financial status. He'd do anything for money. Except actually work.

"Did the book sell well?"

I scanned Ron's voice for any trace of sarcasm. It was clean.

"Do you think it sold well?"

Ron shrugged. "People are idiots."

I allowed myself a small smile. "The book never even made it to a first draft."

When I think of Stephen's writing I think too of the infinite monkey theorem. You know the one; a monkey hitting keys at random for an infinite amount of time would produce the work of William Shakespeare. Well, way before the monkey got to the Bard of Avon she churned out the first ten pages of Stephen's book. The monkey would have been embarrassed by it.

"This partner..."

"Former partner." I cut in.

"Is the ghost?"

He was many things. "I didn't kill him."

"Ah, Jen!" Ron sucked the air in through his teeth. "Now I sort of feel like you might have killed him."

He gave a wry little smile. My lips involuntarily mirrored his.

"Ghosting." Ron held up his smart phone. "I googled it." This was how he was going to solve the cryptic crossword. He would ask the internet for help.

"It's the practice of ending a personal relationship with someone suddenly and without explanation."

"It is that." I inhaled the smell of baked goods. It wasn't enough to counteract the bitter taste.

"We were together for seven years."

He didn't ask, Jen. Why are you telling him this?

"My business was actually doing quite well." It was important to me Ron knew that. Important he understood I was not always a failure.

In a digital age where music and books are available for easy download in the comfort of your own home it seemed a growing number of people wanted to step away from instant gratification.

"People wanted the old world charm of perusing books in the comfort of old sofas, with friends." It was taking every ounce of self-regulation I had not to just disparagingly call them hipsters. That was the exact pitch we'd sold to the bank to make the idea sound more reasonable; more grown up.

"Stephen..."

"He of the zombie apocalypse?" Ron interrupted.

Rude.

I nodded. "He wanted to use the profits to fund a year off work so he could write his best seller."

It had been an odd conversation. I had somehow forgotten that Stephen could work. He had wanted to explore his post University options. Stephen hadn't wanted to get stuck in the payday cycle. Unfortunately, that meant I had to.

"He showed me a first draft." There just weren't the words to describe how awful that had been. "I hadn't said no, but I wasn't planning on saying yes. We'd been together a long time. He must have known. He took the money and quite a few of the expensive antique books and no one has heard from him since. The bank foreclosed on the loan shortly after that."

And he took that book Jen, remember, the special one.

"And you don't know where he is?"

"Oh, yeah, sure I do. I just love the dead end job and minimum wage. Being back with my parents is just the cherry on the cake." I shouldn't have called my job dead end. I had to pretend I wanted a future in finance. I couldn't tell Ron that Smiths was the place my dreams had come to die.

Ron continued to look at me expectantly. As though he wanted to hear more of my story and not like he was waiting for any kind of apology.

"Of course I don't know where he is!" I almost spat the words. I was angry at always having to defend myself.

"No one knows. At least no one is admitting to knowing."

I was pretty sure his parents knew. Well, if not knew, had a way of getting in touch with him. Stephen had always been the golden child. The world owed him a living or, at least, in their eyes, I did.

"Didn't you have a contract?" He looked genuinely interested. No hint of judgement in his tone. It felt wrong to be flippant. I usually said, 'no but I have one now. Wanted: dead or alive. Preferably dead'.

"He's." I stopped. So much had changed. "He was, my partner." Boyfriend seemed so inadequate to describe the time Stephen and I had spent together.

"I'm assuming we've split up." I took a deep breath. I tried not to use sarcasm and humour to hide the pain.

"I didn't think we needed a contract. I trusted him." I wanted to cry at my own naivety.

"I'm sorry." Ron genuinely looked it too. People often said they were sorry but moved on with their life unaffected. Ron looked as though he really cared. As though each time he looked at me he'd remember. Caring was so much worse. Caring was a potent reminder of just how much it all mattered. Not just the financial harm but the emotional damage of it all. The feeling I would never trust anyone again.

"You didn't leave me high and dry." I tried to be flippant. "You've nothing to apologise for."

Maybe now Ron knew my tale of woe he wouldn't sack me. That's why I was telling him things I hadn't told anyone else. It would benefit me later. Ron and I didn't have any kind of connection. I was just using him as part of my plan.

"No one else knows." I was too humiliated to tell anyone.

"They won't hear it from me." Ron's face was so eager and sincere. I almost believed him. I wanted to believe him. As though, if Ron kept his word my faith in humanity could be restored.

For a few moments I couldn't think of a thing to say. For a few moments there was nothing but silence.

"Come on." Ron nodded to the Bakehouse. "Let me buy you lunch."

CHAPTER 7

I should have said no. I should have had more dignity than to accept charity but, if this is rock bottom at least they have proper coffee and a decent Danish pastry.

"I've never been here before." Ron looked around The Bakehouse.

I could offer to pay half the bill. I'd have to spend the rest of the afternoon washing dishes but that was arguably more useful than what I had planned. (A quick nap in the stationary cupboard - if you're interested.)

"I don't know why I told you any of that."

Usually successful people made me feel more inadequate. Ron, for a man everyone seemed pretty terrified of, was remarkably easy to talk to. He had an openness; a quietness that was both uncomfortable and settling. I'm sure this will all be written up in my personnel file but, what the heck. Neil had already amassed quite the character assassination and nothing could be as damning as the past six months.

"Life has ups and downs." Ron glanced briefly at the menu and ordered a boring old salad. In a place filled with all kinds of baked goodness the man opts for a salad. That had to be some kind of criteria on a psychopath test.

'Ups and downs'. As though that platitude could go any way to describing the apocalypse. As though any words could.

The waiter looked at me expectantly. As if I was the kind of person who could quickly look at a menu and just as easily decide I wanted the salad. As though I had so little hope left in my life.

I wanted a cinnamon swirl. However, this was a lunch for grown-ups. Grown-ups don't have cake for lunch. One of my many flaws was I rarely lived life as a grown up. A grown-up would have insisted on a contract; even with the person they trusted most in the world. It wouldn't have mattered they were in love, or they planned to marry and have children. The time spent together was irrelevant. A grown-up would have protected themself. A grown-up would have the salad. My stomach sank.

"The doctor said I've to watch my cholesterol." Ron appeared to sense my hesitation. "It would be a great pleasure if you ordered the unhealthiest thing on the menu."

"So you don't care about my cholesterol?"

There it was again. Another smile. I was relieved my facial muscles still knew how to form the gesture.

"I'll have the cinnamon bun, please."

The waiter nodded. He didn't care. He'd never cared. Mum's little mantra; 'People don't think as much as you give them credit for, love.' Of course, that sage advice was for much smaller personal disasters like coming out of the loo with your knickers tucked into your skirt and toilet roll stuck to your shoe – again. That's another one of my terrible faults; I never learn. So many of life's disasters could have been avoided if only I had taken a moment to stop and think. My head was always clouded with a hundred other thoughts like, do badgers have knees?

"I don't remember you." I thought I'd known all my customers. Particularly the kind ones. "When were you in the shop?"

Ron was most definitely not a hipster. He didn't wear ridiculous clothes or sport the unhygienic, tic infested facial hair that defined our customer base. Stephen had longed to be one of the trendy elite but he couldn't even commit to growing a beard. He envied our clientele and took it really badly any time I wanted to break the monotony of the day with a quick round of 'hipster or homeless'.

No, there wasn't any monotony in the day. The Bookshop was successful. That time in my life was sacred. It would be the period of my existence that formed the yard stick for all that followed. Everything else would fall short. I wasn't exhausted, frustrated, crippled with anxiety and lonely.

"I was hardly ever in the shop. Sorry." People always apologised as though their lack of custom had led directly to the closure. "I saw you one day, briefly when I was in between meetings. I remember faces."

I wanted him to say pretty ones. Weird. He was old enough to be my father, and I had sworn off men. Still, any port in a storm and a compliment would still be a compliment.

It would be seedy though. A much older man, buying lunch for a junior employee; even if that is a junior is closer to 40 than 14. I'm pretty sure Dave is younger than me. He doesn't look it, sure, but that's the curse of male pattern baldness.

"People came in a lot to kill time." Possibly after killing people. Honestly, you want to have seen some of them.

"It must have been Mr. Zombie Apocalypse who served me."

"Well, remember that face and let the Police know."

I watched Ron's sad salad be deposited down in front of him.

"Stephen hardly ever worked in the shop." He preferred spending the money to making it. I'd thought for weeks he'd been helping himself from the cash register.

"What did you buy?"

"I don't remember." Ron shuffled awkwardly in his chair.

It might have been food envy. My cinnamon bun had been placed on the table between us.

Ron probably bought nothing from the shop. He was probably just in out of the rain. Like all of the others. I could have called him out on it. Only, Ron could then have justifiably called me out on the monthly attendance money his firm donated towards my crippling debt repayment plan.

"That looks…" Ron tried to find words for the cream cheese soaked delight.

"Amazing." I offered.

"Sure." His tone indicated he preferred the salad.

Sugar; another unhealthy relationship to add to the list. Whilst I was eating my beautiful cake I could forget the Police thought Stephen and I had orchestrated it all. A few of them still do. Others had seen the puffy eyes and reasoned if we'd planned it together, the deal had changed.

"You're better off without him." Another verbal tic that was offered up as consolation only, again, Ron seemed to mean it. I suppose, just because something sounded like a platitude didn't mean that it wasn't also true.

"He's certainly better off without me."

Stephen had never understood the concept of overheads. He assumed all takings were profit. He would have justified the money he had taken was his own. We'd had to live a lot more frugally whilst the business was taking off. Stephen would have seen any cash he took from the register as compensation for those sacrifices.

Ron had this way of just looking, expecting more.

"It's not true that I'm better off without him. I lost my business, my flat..."

"You lost those things because he stole from you and, if he is capable of that, what more could he have taken over the years?"

Stephen had taken my time too.

"You lost your flat?" Ron seemed surprised.

"I couldn't pay the business loan. I'm technically bankrupt."

Stephen had said we'd get more money from the bank with 'collateral'. He never loved that flat as much as I did. It was never good enough for him.

"My entire life is now literal collateral damage." I tried to laugh but the sound came out harsh.

Ron shifted uncomfortably again in his chair. Successful people were afraid of failure. They seemed to think bad luck was catching. Success, even when you had it, felt fragile.

"You can go if you like. I don't mind." I had the cinnamon bun and so long as he paid the bill before he left, I'd be happy. Well, not happy but, I'd be ok.

Ron looked horrified. He seemed suddenly aware I could read thoughts too.

"I know I don't have a job to go back to. It's ok. The only people I've seen more often than the staff at the bank are those at the Job Centre." And the Police. Don't forget the hours in the Station. Interview after interview. The moment you realised they weren't just taking a statement they were building a case. Against you.

"When your dream is going well you need to protect it. I'm an utter liability." If anything this was a new high. Fired by the ultimate boss. Neil would be proud.

Ron looked serious, and somehow older, although still nowhere near the octogenarian I'd imagined. "This isn't my dream. Well, it was but..." He waved a hand dismissively.

If Ron had a story to tell it was only fair I heard it. Only fair that I had the opportunity to feel less inadequate. I mean, return his compassion.

"You don't need to tell me." I glanced at the world outside The Bakehouse. Ron and I weren't friends. I was just someone he felt sorry for.

"It looks like it might rain later." That's the kind of crap you say to casual acquaintances.

"This was my father's business. It was always just expected I'd take over. So I did. This business has provided well for my family. Life was pretty much as predicted until my wife died."

A potent reminder than even when things were going well events of the universe could just blind side you.

"I'm sorry." I heard the sincerity in my voice.

"It was seven years ago."

Time didn't matter. Not for things like that.

"If I had known I wouldn't have talked about Stephen being a ghost."

"That's what he is to you." Ron sounded pragmatic.

"I thought he was dead." The words fell from my mouth. "When Stephen first disappeared. I thought something terrible must have happened."

I'd called everyone I could think of then, I'd called the Police. It was the Police who discovered the missing money.

"I thought." It's ridiculous, Jen. Don't say it. Ron will think you're ridiculous. "I thought he'd been kidnapped." I looked to the floor, ashamed.

"I thought someone had taken Stephen and the money. It never even occurred to me..."

"You trusted the person that you loved." Ron spoke as though my naivety had been commendable.

When I look back now I can see Stephen had been incrementally leaving for months. He placed more and more distance between us. By the time he finally left Stephen had made me the enemy.

"I know what it feels like to have lost everything, Jen. All the money in the world couldn't save her. I felt so powerless. So helpless. So broken."

It was hard to imagine Ron as any of those things.

"I saw all that again when I looked at you this morning. You hide it better than I did but, it's there."

For one awful moment I thought he was going to start talking to me about religion. You hear that all the time. These successful dissatisfied people finding God and poor God just wishing they'd leave Her alone and stop giving faith and religion such a bad press.

"I'm sorry that your wife died but, I'm not broken." I didn't believe the words. I couldn't make them sound convincing.

The whole world could see it. Strangers in the street stepped out of my way, giving me more space, doing their little part to make the day that bit easier to manage.

"I'm not going to put the boot in, Jen. You're not fired."

"But I've openly told you that I don't even know what I'm supposed to be doing."

Ron shrugged. "You're smart. You'll figure it out. Besides, there's people paid a lot more than you with a lot less of a clue."

I hope he meant Dave.

CHAPTER 8

"How was work, love?"

Mum had made my favourite meal. Well, it was my favourite 'meal' when I was twelve; spaghetti hoops and toast. In her defence I'd hit the dreaded teenage years soon after and discovered boys. Then, I'd gone off to University and only came home following break ups to lick my wounds.

This was a pattern.

No, it wasn't. That was, 'an intrusive thought offering a distorted view of reality'. That was a good article. I should have kept it. I could have bought my own copy had it not been for the terrible life decision; trusting an utter twat.

"Work was fine." I tried to smile brightly.

This job, and all the others that would follow, were my penance for giving up on my dreams. My business had failed, my relationship had failed and independent living had failed. In the next few years I would build a life where none of this could happen again. I would live as cautiously as I had rebuked my parents for. I'd caused them too many sleepless nights with my business loan and mortgage; even when life was going well.

Mum, the eternal optimist, hoped Stephen would return, bringing the money with him.

"Any news?" She asked expectantly every day.

Mum probably even imagined the life Stephen and I had planned could survive this short detour. Stephen was 'a good guy'. 'There had to be some mistake'. I'd thought the same, but I moved on five months ago.

I shook my head and buried the guilt. I was still a failure.

I could have told her about lunch with Ron. I could have told her for twenty minutes I felt like a human being again. I'd laughed, I'd smiled and I'd returned to work feeling a little less broken than before. NB I can say that I'm a bit broken but it's not ok when others (aka Ron) point it out.

Maybe, because Ron was older, he had more of a perspective on life. Ron saw my current situation as a temporary setback. He'd instilled a little of his confidence that things would take an upward turn. Instead, I said nothing. My life was up for public inspection. Those stolen twenty minutes could just be mine. Reality would kick in soon.

"I've made you a packed lunch for tomorrow."

There it was. Tomorrow. Work felt more tortuous that before. Taking money under false pretences from a faceless corporation was fine. Taking it from someone you knew and liked was unacceptable. Not that I liked Ron. He was a man, and those treacherous snakes were strictly off limits.

I'd give it another month a Smiths. Neil should be back to full time work by then. His scorched eyebrows will have most definitely grown back. He'll be well and truly up to the challenge of finding me a new job. He might even be pleased to see me after all this time.

"Thanks Mum."

Before Stephen ran off I was planning on booking Mum and Dad a little surprise break. They'd aged significantly in the past six months. That was my fault too.

Before Stephen. BS. That's what all of this was.

"It's going to be ok, love." Mum pulled out her trusted mantra. She had no idea how, other than the miraculous appearance of Stephen, but it was comforting, and frustrating to hear.

I nodded. I pretended I believed her. It wasn't just the business. It wasn't just the debt. I'd lost Stephen. I'd loved him and, even though I never allowed myself to think it; I missed him. The nights were long and the bed was lonely. His absence made ever more poignant by the growing realisation I'd never trust another man. I'd tried to fancy women but it just wasn't happening. I'd spent an hour trying to long for Jennifer Aniston. Nothing.

Stephen had been my first real love. I thought he was my soul mate. For a few seconds each morning I could almost convince myself it had been a terrible dream but, I woke each day back into the nightmare. I was broken. Ron had seen it at first glance. Surely my own mother saw it too.

"Carol still wants to meet." Mum was apologetic in tone.

Carol, my fiercely ambitious and successful cousin, had been relentlessly tracking me since the news broke. This current fall from grace would be the ultimate opportunity to gloat.

"She's going to come around this weekend with Alice. I'm so sorry, love. I couldn't think of anymore excuses."

Carol and Alice, the nation's power couple, would be full of helpful advice. Helpful advice about what I should have done. That's all anyone had. Nothing about how to keep moving forward. Nothing about how to rebuild a life that had ended. No one had the answer to that. That's why we all had to focus on the past. The future was just existence.

"It's ok." I tried to sound convincing.

It wasn't.

CHAPTER 9

"Nice weekend plans?" Janice smiled broadly. It looked more like a growl. She'd been much more positive towards me since I had 'scored her some one-on-one time with Ron.'

"Why are you two suddenly best friends?" Dave looked suspicious.

"I helped her score with Ron." I murmured; conscious he was within earshot.

Apparently the most recent hobby horse was 'the public face of the organisation'. Janice had it in her head Ron was looking for some kind of pin up girl and she was destined for the spot. Apparently, the company had 'an image problem'. It was the swankiest office I'd seen. All sleek and futuristic. I hoped there weren't factories in developing countries making products these finance people need like, I don't know, calculators. Or, maybe an abacus.

"Janice, what is the plural of abacus?"

"I don't know." As part of her new positive attitude Janice responded to all of my questions.

"Abacuses or abaci." Ron didn't look up from the spreadsheets. I wasn't aware that he'd even been listening.

"What's our image problem?" I lowered my voice in the hope that only Janice could hear.

Someone had spray painted, 'wanker' across the building last week. Dave said I was off the hook because it was done first thing in the morning and I'd still be in bed thinking up an excuse for why I was late. Oh how I laughed. Not. Dave didn't appreciate how hard it was to get out of bed. Then, to come up with inventive excuses such as, 'the bus was delayed because it hit a giraffe'.

Dave was the master of the follow up question. 'What the hell was a giraffe doing in the High Street?' That vein in his temple bulged, threatening to explode.

Honestly, anyone would think he didn't believe me. 'It's 2017, Dave. Giraffe's can go anywhere.'

'It's 2018!' He'd stormed off and slammed the office door. Such a bloody diva.

Dave glanced anxiously at Ron who had his head in some kind of ledger.

"Is it him?" I whispered. "Has he done something hellish?"

"I asked if you had nice weekend plans." Janice's voice impatient again. Our new found friendship was taking its toll.

"Nope." I hoped that would be an end to the 'weekend conversation'. I wanted to take some time in this busy morning of making tea to explain to Dave that Janice and I were getting on better now that our menstrual cycles had synced. I didn't want to have to try and explain the Stepford wives (Alice and Carol). Until now there had been an implicit rule that no one asked me about life outside of these walls. To their credit I think Janice and Dave thought it would implicate them in some kind of crime. They would have been right too.

Janice looked at me expectantly.

"What about you, Janice?" The verbal tic escaped. "What are your weekend plans?"

This was a conversation dictated by social convention rather than genuine interest. Janice could only be having all the make-up sand blasted off. I assumed that was her usual weekend plans. I bet her head was a lot smaller without it.

"What is this?" Ron pointed to something on the computer screen.

Crap. My humorous 'percentage of the chart that looks like Pac man' had made it into the quarterly reports - again.

"That's just a joke, Mr. Smith." Dave's stammered. "I use it in my induction training. It's an eighties computer game character."

Dave appeared more distracted by Janice than angry at me.

"What eighties is that, Dave?"

He ignored the provocation.

"Geoff and I are going wild camping." Janice beamed.

Dave, much to her annoyance, grunted and smirked.

Janice only really discussed her 'personal life' (stream of sexual encounters) when Dave was around. Even her extra-curricular activities were designed to underline she was a team player.

"So, no then." I murmured.

Ron laughed, and then pretended to cough. He caught my eye and smiled.

Ron seemed to be taking an intense interest in our little department. Maybe Janice and Dave were a lot more important than I gave them credit for.

"It's getting back to nature." Janice folded her arms frustrated by Dave's apparent disinterest. I wondered how those nails were going to hold up in the wild.

"It's burying your own crap in the woods."

I didn't want to talk about the weekend with these people. I hated it here but, I hated it everywhere. Being with people was hard, being alone was hard; life was just hard. Besides, thinking about the weekend wasn't living in the present. The weekend, in particular, was going to be hell. Weekends were always hell. No money. No friends. Just hours of wandering around garden centres with the parentals looking for perfect hydrangeas. Full disclosure, I don't even know what a hydrangea is.

"That's not what wild camping is, is it?" Janice grabbed her phone to seek solace and advice from the Great Lord Google.

I watched her scan the screen with increasing concern. She tried to frown but all the muscles in her face were held in place by the million layers of foundation. Janice had inadvertently created an amazing poker face.

'Wild camping' was still going to be more fun than a lunch date with Carol and Alice. Stereo smugness and learned compassion.

"Which one is Geoff?" I tried to recall the inane drivel Janice had spouted into our ears.

Janice had been internet dating for a while. It was a matter of some concern the men she opted for. There's a slim line between an e-fit and a profile picture. I know you shouldn't judge a book by its cover but, if I had to draw a sex offender often those pictures were pretty much what I'd draw. Of course, I'm opposed to victim blaming but, if Janice was murdered by one of those reprobates, that was on her. Those people didn't even look normal. I wanted to say something but hesitated, thinking of Stephen. Monsters looked just like everyone else.

CHAPTER 10

"Do you have any plans this weekend?" Ron appeared whilst I was making my seventeenth coffee of the day.

Ron's presence in our office felt like when the Head Teacher took the naughty class in school. I was exhausted pretending to be busy.

"I have a booking for Hype on Saturday." Ron volunteered. "It's that new restaurant in town."

"Wow! Way to rub it in." Hype had a three month waiting list and even then, only if you knew the right people.

I didn't.

I'd have to sell an organ just to pay for a round of drinks. Just a little organ though; like an appendix or tonsils. At least I had no friends to go with. I'd ostracised them. I didn't have anyone I had to fool into believing I was still cool.

No, that's not what happened. The breakdown of those relationships wasn't my fault. Those friends dumped me when life fell apart. Funtime Frakies. Besides, life changes when you get a partner and Stephen wasn't particularly well liked. Some of the friends left before he did.

"Are tonsils an organ?" That wasn't what I'd intended to say.

"I don't know." Ron reacted as though the question was perfectly reasonable. "My daughter was supposed to be coming with me but the little one has the pox."

"Gross." I shouldn't have to listen to that before lunch.

"Chicken pox." He clarified.

"Still gross."

"It would be a shame to waste the reservation."

"It would be a shame indeed."

He has a Grandson.

"To have your problems." I tried to move past him, even more irritated than before.

"No, I mean you should come with me?"

"Should?"

"Sorry." Ron pulled a face. "Absolutely no obligation. It was just a thought. You seemed..." He paused diplomatically. "Apprehensive about your weekend plans. I have a reservation at Hype and no one to go with. I wondered if you would like to come with me."

"If I say no would it impact on the cataclysmic rise I'm likely to have in your organisation?"

He laughed. If you ask me he laughed a little too hard. "Erm, no."

Why did he want me to go to Hype? I hadn't asked that out loud. Something about looking a gift horse in the mouth. Dad always says, 'if it seems too good to be true it probably is' (usually after he's fallen for another internet scam). I could probably pay the bank back by scamming Dad alone. Perhaps vulnerability to charlatans is a genetic trait. Ron might be asking me out only to harvest my organs. I should ask him why he's inviting me. It's a reasonable question

"The pie chart was mine." I didn't have to admit it. I hadn't intended to say it either. Only, it was beyond decent of Dave to take the blame.

"I put it in the report to wind Dave and Janice up. I thought I'd deleted it." I hadn't. I put the chat in and I thought no more about it.

Ron looked as though another part of the puzzle had just fallen into place.

"Dave takes his job really seriously. He's one of the good guys."

Wow. Did I really believe that?

"I heard he has a good mentor." Ron smiled. Reminding us both that I had indeed told him that I was Dave's boss.

"So, what about this Hype reservation?" He asked again.

"You seem to have missed the fact that I'm legally bankrupt." I can't be having stolen glances across the office with someone's Papa.

69

No, that wasn't what was happening. Only, I didn't know what was happening. Part of my brain is completely consumed by thinking about the role of the tonsils in human anatomy.

Ron looked concerned. "It was only technically bankrupt on Tuesday."

"It's official now." A shiny red letter had come through the post this morning. Redirected from the flat; the one that had been repossessed by the very people sending the letter.

Oddly, we high fived. Clinking our coffee mugs together in mock celebration.

"We should commiserate." He looked away. Embarrassed or, something else.

"This would be my treat."

It was the something else that puzzled me.

"I couldn't. It's not right. I'm not a charity case."

I was already taking a monthly wage for, well, that's just it. I was taking the money to pay off my debts. I have no idea why they were so freely giving it to me. True, it wasn't much of a wage and I was miserable whilst here but, a girl's got to have principles.

"Truth is," Ron looked around. "You'd be doing me a massive favour. Everyone I know has eaten there. I'm beginning to look really unhip." Ron mocked concern. I imagined him to be a man who cared very little for what people thought.

I laughed.

No, no laughing. No weakening of resolve. I already had the charity cheese sandwiches for lunch and I am fairly confident that bread was mouldy.

"Take a night off punishing yourself for someone else's mistake. Then," he proceeded cautiously, "when you get your half of the millions that any book about a zombie apocalypse is bound to make, you can treat me."

"That's not funny." Although it was, a bit.

I had to say no. We both knew I'd never repay him. I was down and this time I was out. Only, Carol and Alice's faces were swimming before my eyes, waiting for their turn to pass judgement. I didn't know if I had it in me to face another forensic dissection of my life. If lunch the other day was anything to go by Ron is actually really good fun. What the hell, I was probably being groomed and may end up being sold into slavery but I deserved a treat (the dinner out, not the exploitation. I had that nailed).

"I could pick you up." Ron saw I was beginning to waiver.

"No, it's ok." I thought of the parental with their noses pressed against the window as they watched a man who was in their class at the school (had they gone to a better school) taking me out on a date.

No. It wasn't a date. It was. Well, I don't know what it was but, I guessed I was about to find out.

"I'll meet you there."

CHAPTER 11

"Out?" Mum couldn't have been more surprised if I'd announced I was going on a daytrip to the moon.

"You're going out?" She repeated the words as if hoping they would make sense the second time around.

"A friend asked me for dinner." It wasn't much of an explanation.

"Which friend?" Mum really had missed her calling as a detective or a lawyer.

"You don't know him."

"A male friend." She smiled. The first genuine smile I'd seen in months. There were loads of forced, anxious, 'it's going to be alright, love' smiles where she'd look at Dad for reinforcement but his face kept yelling, 'na, you're well and truly fecked." (He still doesn't like to swear in front of me, even non-verbally).

"A date?" She asked hopefully. Her eyes widened in anticipation. As her only daughter I should be married, with children. Children she could babysit when I was at work for someone else. Risk free. Good pension and benefits. Nine 'til five. The job at Smiths was killing my soul but she had described it on the phone as, 'a step in the right direction'. Maybe she was right. If that direction was off a cliff.

"It's not like that." I couldn't explain why it wasn't 'like that'. To mention either Ron's age or status in the organisation was likely to result in another trip to HR and they were tiring of my antics more quickly than the Job Centre had. The HR team at Smiths most definitely had a sense of humour bypass. Perhaps that was an essential requirement in the job description. I wondered if I could have a look at mine. It seemed wrong now to be taking money under false pretences.

"You shaved your legs." Mum had a way of just knowing these things.

"That was for me."

Only, shaving my legs didn't make me feel better. I had to buy the cheap razors. I looked like I'd been self harming and probably had tetanus.

"We're just friends. Someone let him down for the reservation and it's really hard to get in."

I felt like a teenager again. Not lying exactly, just concealing the truth. For example, the OAP I was going to dinner with was the boss, his daughter had let him down, he was very attractive but I can say that as I am a sexless human and he's a grandfather. A good bout of nookie could see him into the next world. Even though he looked as though he had stamina... I should just call and say I was sick. The 'not a date' was getting very complicated.

"I'm thinking of becoming a nun." I announced to reinforce my celibate status.

Mum laughed. I don't know why. I'd make a good nun. If it wasn't a silent order. And they allowed a bit of swearing. And vengeance. Because so help me God if Stephen isn't dead I might just bloody kill him. I'd even thought about how... And, what I'd do with the body. Can't say that out loud though. The word premediated would then be banded around a courtroom.

Mum smiled again. "It sounds like a date."

In that it involved me and a male. It had to be date. There had to be some hope left in the world for her.

"Is it one of those nice Police men?"

"I haven't met any nice Police men." It was inconceivable to Mum that anyone would think me complicit in Stephen's crime. Even when I was taken away in the back of a squad car for a three hour interrogation.

"I don't have to go. This leaves you with Carol and Alice." I felt guilty. Well, I felt relieved but I understood that I should have felt guilty.

"She's my niece." Mum sounded unconvincing." You enjoy your date."

"It's not a date!" I hollered as I ran for the bus. I wanted to hang around and emphasise the platonic nature of the event but I'd be late.

By the time I got home Mum would have me married off to the mystery man. That would be a neat little ending. The woes of one man resolved by another. It was wrong to give her that hope but, if I was going to have the night off crippling anxiety, why couldn't she?

Mum's questions and hope made me anxious. I told myself Ron would know it wasn't a date. Successful men don't date drop outs. This was just friends. Charity... So why was I wearing my good underwear. Again, that was for me. I had very few occasions to wear my good underwear now Jen was 'man free'. Only, when I'd had a few drinks, drunk Jen can be kinda sloppy.

Poor old drunk Jen. She'd taken a lot of slack for bad decisions back in the day. It was sober Jen who had caused this little debacle.

I almost resented saying I'd meet Ron at Hype. That meant another bus trip into town. Hype was near my flat too. My old flat. I could feel it pull me back. If I wasn't running late I'd have tortured myself by walking past. Smiths was on the opposite side of town. I never had to pass where my little world imploded. I tried to pretend it didn't exist but somewhere, less than a mile from where I stood, other people were living bits of my life. Someone was living in my old flat. Someone else was working in what had been my shop. Someone else may be sleeping with my boyfriend. Ex-boyfriend. I felt the blood drain from my face and I wanted to cry. This was a bad idea. The worst one yet but, I'd just come face to face with the stuck up 'door bitch' from Hype. It was too late to back out now.

"Can I help you?" The 'host' (aka beautiful but too clumsy to carry plates waitress) approached.

It was like that scene in Pretty Woman where the uptight woman wouldn't let Julia Roberts buy humpty clothes from her very 80s boutique.

Never has a look screamed, 'I think you want the soup kitchen' more than the one the door bitch shot me.

I took a deep breath and tried to brazen it all out. This was worse than having someone look into my soul and see the darkness. These people were trained to see your bank balance and credit rating like an aura. I took another deep breath to try to explain something I didn't understand; why I was here.

CHAPTER 12

Hype was as swanky as people implied. No one would come right out and say they were impressed. That would ruin the game of showing how amazingly cultured and sophisticated we all are and shatter the illusion nothing can impress us.

I was greeted with borderline contempt by Door Bitch. My dress was last seasons. Not a timeless classic either. Proper fast fashion tat.

"I'm meeting a friend." I finally managed.

By this point the manager had appeared to deal with the mute at the door. I'd rehearsed the words on the way here. Well, I'd rehearsed them once I'd finally calmed myself down from being convinced I one hundred and ten per cent had lock jaw from the nicks from the cheap razors and should probably just go to A & E.

I'd thought about backing out. I could have text Ron stating I'd forgotten I usually man a helpline for the chronically unlucky; they call me to hear my story and feel good about life.

I hadn't thought I'd be so anxious walking into a restaurant alone. I hadn't been out with another man in over seven years. Not that this was 'out' but, you know what I mean. I didn't think I'd be so nervous either. Then, when my eyes met his - I wasn't. It was a relief to find Ron's friendly face in what felt like a hostile crowd.

He smiled and I felt more at ease.

Ron stood up as I was shown to the table. There's something alluring about an older man. One who would arrive early to ensure you didn't have to wait at the bar alone. A man whose idea of a romantic night out didn't include a trip to McDonald's and a PlayStation. Still, that night wasn't all that bad. I was a bit drunk and showing off my flare for improvised dancing. The Night Manager at McDonald's said I had 'moves'.

"You look beautiful." Ron smiled again, relieved. I wondered if he had considered flaky Jen would ditch him.

I would need to pluck up the courage to remind him this wasn't a date. I thought I'd established that when I had said I would meet him here. It definitely wasn't just to hide him from my parents. Or, to ensure no one from work spotted us. I glanced anxiously around.

Weekend Ron looked different. Jeans and a sports jacket. Shirt, no tie. Unthinkable. The Head Teacher on dress down day, or a dog walking in high heels and wearing a trilby.

"Thanks." No! I was supposed to be setting boundaries. "You look like its casual Friday." That might just have been rude.

Ron laughed and ordered another drink.

"I'm glad you came."

Way to admit vulnerability.

"You thought I might stand you up?" No, Jen. This isn't a date. You can't be saying things like that.

"Worse. I was worried you might ghost me."

"It was either this or dinner with my cousin and her wife. They've been looking forward to pointing out my failings for months but I've successfully managed to avoid them."

"There are other things you could have done tonight." Ron appeared grateful that I was here. I appreciated that he thought I had options.

"You shouldn't be hiding." He offered me the drinks menu. Big mistake usually but, having no money really made you pay attention to the price of things. And, sadly, I mean literally no money. One bottle of wine here was two credit card payments in the real world. A world that felt very far away.

"I'm ok, thanks." I tried not to look at the menu. It was a new tactic in life. If you didn't look you couldn't see what you were missing.

"She'll have a Pink Flamingo." Ron called to the waiter. He turned to me and whispered "The woman at the next table ordered one and I really wanted to have a look."

"This isn't the dark ages. You can't just order for me."
I heard the anger in my voice. Since Stephen's betrayal
it was always so close to the surface. So ready to become
uncontrollable rage.

'She'll have the pink flamingo'.

Bloody men! Good. I'm glad that he annoyed me.
That could relieve some of the guilt. No, not guilt. Why
would I feel guilty? Stephen literally owed me thousands
of pounds. I shouldn't feel guilty for seeing another man.
It's not that I was going behind his back. I didn't know
where Stephen's back was.

Ron shrugged. "You'll be quicker off the mark next
time. There's also something called a Firecracker. That
one has milk." He pulled a dramatically disgusted face
and my anger dissipated.

The Pink Flamingo was one of the most expensive
drinks on their menu.

Ron was a rescuer. He'd seen I was embarrassed
about ordering a drink and he'd helped. Maybe that was
why I was here tonight. I was his next project; a fixer
upper. This was my generations *My Fair Lady*. I would be
taken to some conference and paraded around as I
recited something to do with the FTSE. I wish I knew
something about finance. It would really have helped
with that analogy.

"How's your grandchild?" I should have thought of
something more intelligent to say on the way over. Next
I'll be asking him when he gets his pension. Or, if I do get

done for fraud, whether I could offset tonight as volunteer work for Age Concern.

No Jen, don't say anything cray cray; (my parents have never liked calling me 'crazy'). 'Cray cray' is their pet term for my 'unique and creative outlook on life'. AKA when I say 'mental things'; Carol had less concern for politically correct terminology.

"The one ridden with the pox?"

"I've had their home burnt to the ground. It's the only way to deal with the infestation." He smiled as a luminous bright drink was deposited in front of me in what looked to be an old jam jar. It's amazing the impact of poverty on such hipster nonsense. I understood immediately that whatever they'd serve my dinner on it sure as hell wouldn't be a plate.

"There's no real flamingo in this, right?"

CHAPTER 13

Ron was amazing. He was confident, funny, and articulate. He made me feel completely at ease. We'd had a few curious glances throughout the evening from onlookers speculating on nature of our relationship. I hadn't speculated since I'd arrived. No tension. No awkward silences. All we wanted from each other was uncomplicated company. Things had been increasingly complicated with Stephen. It was almost a relief when he left. *No, I was heartbroken, remember?* I'd cried for weeks about the money. I mean, the betrayal. I was just trying to 'reframe'. That means think positively about the negative thing.

The alcohol soothed my weary mind. If I wasn't careful this could become another relationship to add to the unhealthy list. If I had money I'd definitely drink more. Not enough to be drunk; just enough to be tipsy. Tipsy made me more optimistic. If that feeling could be bottled I'd buy it by the case; but only when it was on special offer.

"You should smile more often. It makes the world feel calmer." Ron looked at me, thoughtfully. Clearly I continued to fascinate him. He'd lose interest once he figured me out. It's amazing how quickly an attraction to 'quirky' led to frustration. Or, it attracts the wrong kind of people. It attracts people who think there's a quick buck to be made in books about zombie apocalypses.

"You're not supposed to tell women to smile more." I stood up for my feminist values.

"Are you trying to tell me people are afraid of me? That I'm less scary when I smile. Would you have said any of that if I was a man?"

"I don't think you're at all scary."

"But others do?"

Ron laughed. "I would like to object." He held his hands up in submission.

I think I'd made Dave cry once in the early days.

"My cousin Carol says I have resting bitch face."

"You don't."

I had the wonderful feeling that Ron admired my face.

"My Mum thought RBF it meant really bright future." I laughed. "I don't have one of those either."

I put the drink down. That was probably enough of the old truth serum.

"I don't believe that. I hope you don't either." Ron spoke as if he had some kind of knowledge as to how my life would turn out. Maybe that's what he was. A message from the future. A sign not to give up hope.

"At least I won't be going to prison." I hadn't thought that was a possibility until the lawyer told me that it was highly unlikely. "It would have been free digs though." An escape from the Princess bed at my parents.

"You thought you would be charged?"

"Nope, but then I didn't think the Police were working on theory Stephen and I had been in it together."

I would have had to have been a convincing liar. When I started to cry that night I thought I would never stop. It was a relief to my parents when the tears came. I had been mute for two hours with the shock.

"I wasn't always like this. People used to like me. I used to like myself."

Ron would remember the carefree girl from the shop. Mum said I idealised the place and it wasn't, 'all that' but, it was better than this. Well, maybe not this evening. I hadn't felt this relaxed in years. Owning your own business was stressful. Especially when going it alone.

You weren't supposed to be alone.

"People like you." Ron objected, unconvincingly.

They did, once.

"Not at work they don't."

"They like you fine. They just think you're shiftless." That was hard to argue with. "You know Jen, the world hasn't ended."

"Mine did."

"It only feels that way." Ron never made me feel like a failure. He saw this hell as a temporary blip and gave me some faith that it would pass. He gave me perspective; a man so in control had his life shattered when his wife died. Ron realised, what we all sometimes forget - life is even more fragile that success.

"I lost everything."

"Not everything." Ron prompted. "You have your parents. You have your health. In some of my toughest moments I've ensured I held on to the things that mattered."

"Like the little sports car outside?" He was definitely having a midlife crisis. If anything, that was what tonight was.

"My family. My integrity."

Sure, be noble.

"That car belongs to my daughter."

The car was worth more than my flat. "Is it pox ridden? Should we burn it?"

Ron examined me from over his whisky glass. "I'm only eighty per cent sure you're joking."

"We could split the insurance." I smiled. "Plus, fire is pretty." The bonfire that was my life wasn't.

"I think between us we can figure out a more positive trajectory." Ron sounded as though he was talking about the spreadsheets.

"Put the apocalypse behind me?" It felt like I was going to have to live with those mistakes forever.

'The event' was too non-descript but 'the apocalypse' was perhaps too fatalistic. I needed something more reflective of the magnitude of all and yet, also more containing.

"My own little personal Armageddon."

Just for a second, the power of the events of the past six months diminished.

"It sounds like one of those swanky cocktails." Ron nodded towards another majestic creation with sparklers.

You'd think alcohol and fire would be a bad combination. The antibacterial gel on Neil's desk was engulfed in flames in seconds. I should have reconsidered the sparklers on his birthday cake. I should have remembered too that marzipan is mostly just almonds and almonds are also a nut.

"Or the Pan Galactic Gargle Blaster." The words stung.

"The what?" Ron's eyes twinkled again.

I amused him. The quirky girl always did at the start.

"It doesn't matter." *It does. It always will.*

Ron continued to look at me expectantly.

"It's a drink in my favourite book. It's not important."

Ron leaned back in his chair. "It seems important."

"I had a signed copy of *The Hitchhiker's Guide to the Galaxy*. My Aunt gave it to me on my 12th birthday. It is, was, my prized possession. Stephen took that too." Ron continued to look. I don't know what more he wanted. For a woman adept at changing the subject I was lost for a distraction. It was perplexing how Ron managed to pull the truth buried deep inside.

Maybe he was with the bank. Maybe that's why I was here.

"Of all the things Stephen took that hurt the most. He knew how much it meant to me and he took it anyway."

I could feel the tears sting my eyes. This isn't what Ron wanted. This wasn't what anyone wanted. We were here to enjoy the new hot spot in town. Fun, flippant Jen had been invited to the party and she wasn't known and admired for her depth of conversation.

A few moments silence passed between us. I couldn't look at Ron. I'd lost thousands of pounds, my home and most of my possessions so few people understood the importance of an old book. I could feel the armour of the past few months falling away. I didn't want Ron to see my vulnerability. I didn't want to feel it.

Ron reached out. He placed his hand gently on mine. Forcing me to look up.

"You do understand Jen, this isn't about the book?"

How could he say that? How could anyone say that? Why did they all keep saying it?

I felt my bravado return. "Show's how little you know me." I picked up the cocktail menu and withdrew my hand. "It's always about the book."

CHAPTER 14

"Of course this is about the book." I snapped again. Frustrated that Ron didn't understand. That no one understood. When I told Mum and Dad how much it upset me they tried to source another. As though my prized possession could be so easily replaced.

Ron awkwardly recounted how his father had been declared bankrupt; twice. I would have asked follow up questions but there was no point in underlining how little I knew about the company. Besides, reading between the lines it sounds as though his father was a complete nightmare. Utterly ruthless. Perhaps that accounted for why Ron was so kind. I tried to put on a hard face each day, but I'd never crack ruthless.

"How long are you planning on coasting along?" Ron casually asked. As though his story of generational wealth was supposed to have inspired me.

"Coasting? Seven years together and Stephen just walked out of my life, taking most of it with him. He never even looked back. No remorse. Nothing."

I hated to be clichéd about giving Stephen the best years of my life. I'd done more than that. I'd given him the best of me.

Surely, if anyone was allowed a bit of coasting it was me. I was healing. Apparently.

"You don't know that." Ron looked more serious. Defensive almost. As though it was I, and not Stephen, who had undermined the whole of mankind.

"He's not here, is he?" I heard the bitterness in my voice. I felt the familiar ball of anger in my stomach. "Not even when there were threats of me going to jail. Not even when I was held in Police custody for six hours with questions being fired at me in all directions."

No wonder people confessed to crimes they didn't commit. I would have said anything just to make it stop.

Ron shook his head. "It was clear you had nothing to do with it."

"Not to them it wasn't." I wasn't even sure they cared how much I was implicated.

"Here's how much of a walk over I am. I'm actually worried that he might not be ok. What the hell does that make me?"

I couldn't, or wouldn't, fully believe my Stephen had left me so willingly. So finally. So brutally.

"A better person."

"A doormat. I should hate him." I tried to hate him. Every single day I tried.

"I don't think you could hate anyone." Ron looked at me again, too thoughtfully and, again, with too much compassion.

Wrong again. I hated Janice. Stephen was a work in progress.

"I'm getting there."

I hated what he'd done to my life. I hated the anxiety and worry on the faces of my parents. I hated the way he'd made them age. *I hated myself.*

No, that wasn't right. I was the victim. I shouldn't blame me, the victim. That's not acceptable. Even though I'd described Janice as 'serial killer fodder' to Dave I generally abhorred victim blaming.

"Do I look like a woman with thousands of pounds stashed under my bed?" I laughed, bitterly. "My single princess bed that I insisted my parents buy when I was nine. A bed so expensive, and remarkably sturdy, they won't get rid of it."

This is why I didn't drink. Alcohol erodes the little self-regulation I had.

Ron shifted awkwardly in his chair. Maybe because wealthy people hated talking about money. Maybe because my entire ensemble tonight screamed 'poverty, bankrupt, broken'... Maybe he didn't want to think about my bed.

I blushed, "Sorry."

I hadn't wanted to make Ron feel awkward or distant. For a few moments he'd drifted away. Maybe I was right

90

about the early onset dementia. I could use that to my advantage. He would forget about tonight.

Ron gave me what I can only assume was an appraising look. "Was it easy to set yourself up in business?"

"No." I didn't have his advantages. I grew up in a council house on an estate. No hereditary company for Jen.

"Were there ever times when money was so short you thought you were going to have to pack it all in?"

"Of course." All businesses have that.

"So, what makes this any different?"

CHAPTER 15

Mum eyed me up and down. "Have you done something with your hair?"

"No." She'd been at this all morning.

"You look different." Mum gasped. "You've had sex?"

"No!" I took a deep breath and tried to divert her. "Never, Mum. Honest. I'm still a virgin. When are we going to have that special talk?"

She handed me a plate of toast. "We used to talk about everything."

"Not sex!" We were never that close. Were we? Even if there had been a night of wild passion it wasn't something I'd chat about over cornflakes with my Mum.

"How were Carol and Alice?" I tried to change the subject.

"How are they always?" Mum sighed. She would not want to speak ill of her sister's child but there was little positive that could be said.

"I heard they're getting an allotment." They'd been on the waiting list for several years. It irked Carol that with all her connections the Horticultural Club did not permit any queue jumping.

"Stop trying to change the subject."

"I'm just a bit tired." I'd got home late, well early, this morning.

"You're Dad waited up. He was getting worried."

"I'm thirty-four."

"You could be a hundred and four and he would still wait up for you."

That felt unlikely.

"Sorry. I won't stay out that late again."

"Love, you just told me. You're thirty-four. Let your Dad stay up. Don't you be cutting your night short." She looked at me expectantly.

"So you had a nice time with the gentleman?"

"Mum." She always made it sound like we lived in Victorian England.

She needed more information.

"You know what those strip clubs are like. Open all hours."

She shrugged. "One way to make money I suppose."

Ron and I hadn't noticed the restaurant empty around us. We'd spent the night talking about everything and nothing. There was no ground that couldn't be trespassed. I'd shown Ron the worst of myself and he'd accepted it; uncritically and without judgement. I used to think men and women couldn't be friends. When you accept life as a singleton it opens up a world of new possibilities. We had a relationship free of any sexual tension. Ron had lived an entire lifetime with someone else. He had his own child; his child had her own child. Last night was absolutely platonic, only... There was one moment.

Ron insisted on accompanying me home. It probably was overkill, even in this day and age, but I hadn't really wanted the evening to end. He walked me to the door whilst the taxi waited on the corner. I'd forgotten what it was like to have money to burn.

I was beyond tipsy and it was all beginning to feel a bit Jane Austin, which made me giggle. Ron wiped the hair from my face and looked deep into my eyes. I felt something life very rarely granted; silence. Usually I have a whole manner of random thoughts floating around my brain like, I wonder if fish have knees. Or would I rather have a pet elephant or buffalo? Sometimes I make a list to help me decide. Yet, in that moment, there was nothing. Ron looked into the depths of my soul and saw the person I was. The nice one I had trapped deep inside for being so naive, for trusting the wrong man, for ruining her life. He saw the heartbreak, the disappointment and the utter sense of despair and tolerated all that I'd found to be unbearable.

'You're a smart woman, Jennifer Blake. You're funny and you're stronger than you think. You'll get through this.'

'I'm a wash out.' I whispered, so only he could hear my disappointment.

'No.' Ron stroked my face. 'You're burnt out.'

'That's so much better.'

'A Phoenix always rises from its own ashes. Bolder, brighter, stronger.' He leaned his head against mine and took a deep breath. In that moment he was breathing for us both.

The world disappeared around us and for a few seconds we were all that existed. Frozen in time. No past, no future; just here, just now. The problems and the pains of the past few months were held in a vacuum somewhere else. I felt lighter. The tension flowed from my muscles. I looked deep into his eyes and felt understood.

I don't know how long we stood there. The silence was only broken when the taxi driver sounded his horn. Ron sighed, moving his head slightly to the side, scowling at the noise that had broken this perfect moment of peace.

'I had better go.' He whispered. There was a reluctance to his tone.

I wondered what I would have done had my parents not been asleep inside. Or, if the taxi had stopped at his place first. Well, let's face it, given the state of my finances I'd have had to sleep with the taxi driver in lieu of payment.

I nodded, and reluctantly watched him go.

Mum was right about one thing. Something had changed. Some of the pain and worry from the past six months had been left in that vacuum.

CHAPTER 16

"Has he called?" Mum was desperate for a conventionally happy ending. One she could explain to her friends because she herself understood it.

She wouldn't have understood Ron. I didn't understand Ron.

"It wasn't a date." I continued to protest, even though I was no longer quite sure what it had been.

"Alice was impressed you'd managed to get a table at Hype."

I'd managed nothing but was relieved that Mum continued to draw some sense of pride from my existence.

"What was it like?"

Appropriately named. The hype around the place was better than the food. Marketing genius.

"Yeah, it was nice." I didn't want to sound ungrateful.

I'd have felt too old if I was honest and said the music was too loud. It could have made conversation hard.

Thankfully, we had a table secreted at the back away from the live DJ. I only just considered that may have been by design. Ron could have been as anxious as I was that we were seen together. When I placed that thought in his head I was mortified by it.

"Carol hasn't managed to get a table." Mum beamed. "She's desperate to write up a blog on the place."

I'm fairly confident the grammar in that sentence was all wrong.

Carol, like half of the world, was a blogger. A 'self confessed foodie. With a face you'd never tire of punching'. Ok, I added the last part.

"Was it as impressive as they seem to think?"

"I imagine the bill was impressive."

"He paid?" Mum liked it when we all performed assigned gender roles. I'm not sure when the roles were assigned, or by whom but it seemed Mum's world was governed by that unwritten code.

Mum would have been ecstatic if she had known Ron also walked me to the door. Sure, she proclaimed to be a feminist but Mum still wanted a man to pick up the bill and open all the doors.

Ron had taken the recycled can of beans (what else?) containing the bill and placed his card in without even looking. I could have paid a year's worth of debt, and possibly that of a small African country, as an alternative. So I'd initially repressed the urge to offer him a bag of chips on the way home.

'That was lovely.' I'd smiled woozy from the latest Pink Flamingo (they were weirdly addictive). Then, I couldn't help myself, 'fancy some chips?' To my utter amazement he did. So we left the city's swankiest eatery and queued at the recently re-opened (with the minimal pass in food hygiene standards) 'Plaice2b' (you couldn't make it up). Only, I'm not really sure it was the chips that he wanted.

I should do something nice for Ron. If I decided his taking me to dinner was a nice gesture. People often got the wrong idea about me. As I am often so open about what I say people assume I will be open to other things. Sexual things. Again, it's hard to say for sure, but I'm pretty confident I've been invited into more threesomes that the average person.

"He paid." It felt important I said that. Like the money she'd given me when I really needed it wasn't being squandered.

Mum understood the implication. "You have to start living again, love."

As though it would have been acceptable for me to have picked up the bill.

"I don't have money to live. I just have existence cash."

She shook her head, sadly. As though I was the one to have missed the point.

I hated that Ron paid. I didn't want to feel indebted to him. I couldn't feel indebted to anyone else. My entire life felt like a series of final demands.

Maybe I could bake Ron some biscuits. Thoughtful and, best of all, cheap.

No, I couldn't. I hadn't baked since they closed the shop. It would bring back too many painful memories of having to work all day and bake all night. No, that wasn't the memory. Was it?

"Carol seemed quite taken aback you were working at Smiths." Mum smiled, "a high profile place is it?"

Lunch had of course become dinner because Carol and Alice were so busy and important they always had to re-arrange. The rest of us were just waiting in the wings to be summoned. Carol would have been surprised I had any plans at all.

"No idea." I wondered whether I should tell her about the 'wanker' incident.

Wanker.

As though the, what the hell let's say artist, was talking of a particular person. Perhaps, the person's whose name was emblazoned above the door.

"You know the fast paced work of finance." No one did but, they'd never admit it.

"No, love, I don't."

No one but Mum.

"What is it they do?" She quizzed.

"Mergers and acquisitions." I'd read that on door a somewhere when lost on a general office wander.

Please, have no other follow up questions. I had no idea what either of those words meant but it sounded like the kind of terms that would impress Carol.

Mum smiled again. "If you stick in you can work your way through the ranks."

"Maybe," I had sort of assumed they all had some kind of relevant training. Advanced Countdown, maybe.

Mum radiated hope and happiness. In her mind I would soon have another boyfriend and a better job with far less personal risk. The past six months would be a distant memory and a steep learning curve on the dangers of venturing outside the comfort zone. Maybe Dad would stop hiding in the garage too when life picked up a bit.

"When are you seeing him again?" Mum tried to pretend she hadn't been dying to ask.

"We're just friends, Mum. I'm not ready for another relationship."

I won't be so willingly led to the slaughter. Besides, I couldn't tell her part of me felt guilty. Even though it hadn't been a date, even though it was all 'just friends'. Part of me still felt I was in a relationship with Stephen. Maybe it was because neither of us had any 'closure'. One day, he just never came home. Maybe I needed to have the 'this is the end talk'. Either that or I'd been watching too much daytime TV. Stephen had more of a sense of an ending than me; he must have known he was leaving for weeks.

"Well, love. If we wait until we're ready we'll spend out whole lives waiting."

I'd originally been impressed with her wisdom until I'd found out she had subscribed to an 'inspirational quotes' page on social media. Sure Mum was all sage about relationships but if I'd brought another business venture idea to her she'd have had a stroke. My parents grew up in the golden age of relationships and marriage. It was just expected you would meet someone, marry and have children. The done deal. My generation had so many options Stephen and I hadn't chosen any of them.

Mum could see the distant look appear in my eye and tried to pull me back. "What's the matter, love?" She took my hand and feigned concern. "Was he rubbish in bed?"

"Mum!" I was genuinely horrified.

She just laughed.

CHAPTER 17

"Nice weekend?" Ron held open the side door for me.

"Employees aren't supposed to use this entrance." I smiled and handed him the biscuit tin.

Should it be this nice to see him? A friendly face in Dante's Hell. That's all. However, if this was Hell wouldn't that make him the devil?

"I see our resident artist is back." Workers in boiler suits were out scrubbing the window again.

Ron looked darkly at the graffiti.

"Do we know who the wanker is?" I tried to sound casual. I tried not to make it sound like an accusation.

Ron's face inscrutable. "What is this?" He held up the tin.

"Suspicious package. We need to clear the area and we all need to go home."

I didn't want to go home.

Ron looked quizzically at the tin. I'm not entirely sure how a Power Rangers packed lunch box had made it into my life.

"It's just a thank you for Saturday."

"The bomb might have been the better offering." He looked sadly to the paint resisting the industrial strength cleaner.

Stephen! Of course, the box had to belong to Stephen. He wasn't very good at being a grown-up either. The Peter Pan of his social circle; the traditional scary version who slaughtered the lost boys so they never outgrew him.

"Florentines. My best seller." I sounded proud. It almost hurt.

Ron continued to look at me blankly.

"You're not allergic to nuts, are you?"

Neil was. That was another 'unfortunate incident' cited in his Doctor's note.

"I used to think people came to the shop for the baked goods rather than the books." They didn't always buy books and, come to think of it, we tended to sell more online.

Ron grimaced apologetically, "Cholesterol."

"I never thought..." He'd mentioned the elevated levels the first time we had lunch. That's why he had the salad. I tried to take them back.

"Take the biscuits and lose the hand." He smiled, warmly. Ron appeared more relaxed as we made our way into the building and away from the graffiti.

Out of sight out of mind.

That's not a good approach to life, Jen. Stephen was of the, 'if I don't see the problem, or if I ignore it, then it's not an issue' branch of philosophy. The issues didn't just go away. They got bigger. Then, I had to clean up the mess.

"You bake?" Ron opened the box and peered inside.

"I do lots of things. I have many talents." People often assumed that I bought the biscuits in. I suppose it was a backhanded compliment.

"I don't doubt it." He smiled again.

I was relieved the distant guilty look was gone. For a moment it felt as though there had been some kind of divide between us. Maybe there was. I'm not sure I could be friends with someone who had such a strong adverse reaction to sugar.

"I always came for the books." Ron coughed.

"I thought you said you'd only been there a few times." Maybe Ron, like everyone else, was tired of hearing how magical the dream had been. Only... No, I was just tired and emotional. Making the Florentines was a big thing. I didn't even need to look at the recipe. Not once. I could have made them in my sleep. Sometimes it felt as though I had. I cried a few times back then. I was so tired. My arms ached. Stephen was asleep on the sofa, or watching TV complaining he'd had a long day and the baking was keeping him awake. I'd often been up since six and it was usually well after midnight. Stephen was working far less hours than me and, eventually, he wasn't working at all. Much of the tasks that consumed my day could have been shared. They weren't.

Ron sighed and kissed me gently on the cheek. "Thank you." He reached into the Power Rangers box and removed a Florentine. "Wow! These are amazing."

"Yeah. We had signs up about them in the shop." Pictures on the door too.

I tried to forget the weirdness that had passed between us. Only, people used to come in specially to buy the Florentines. Anyone who knew me from the shop asked about the biscuits before anything else. That's why I had stayed up several nights a week baking them. Odd he should remember me and not the biscuits.

"This does put me back in your debt." Ron cringed at his clumsy words and ploughed on. "I have a ticket for the opera tonight."

"The opera? And what, you want me to phone whoever you are going with and tell them you're sick? Burn the ticket? Burn the theatre?" I shouldn't care who he planned to go to the opera with. Why did I want to know? I couldn't just ask him. That would be weird, right?

"Burning things seems to be your go to solution."

"I told you." I shrugged as though arson was inconsequential. "Fire's pretty."

Maybe Ron had a partner. Of course he had a partner. He was attractive, funny and compassionate.

The only way he'd be single was if he was into some pretty kinky sex stuff.

Like what?

Stop Jen! His daughter is probably older than you. How would you feel if someone your age started dating your dad? Repulsed. But that's because he's my Dad and he's lucky to have Mum.

It would have been weird for us to be out last night if Ron did have a partner. Stephen would never have allowed that. He was too possessive. No, I mean committed. Don't I?

"I was supposed to be going with friends."

"You need new friends." Maybe that's what I was. Good, I could do with new friends. I could do with a friend.

"Have you ever been to the opera?" Ron pulled me back from the all consuming past.

My head was like a warped magic ball. Each time I glanced at the past I had to decide whether it was the memory, or my recollection of it, that was distorted.

"Have I ever been to the opera?" I made a pretence of giving the question serious consideration. "No, Mr. Smith. I would rather watch paint dry."

"Don't call me Mr. Smith."

Ron hadn't objected when Dave did it.

"How do you know you don't like the opera if you've never been?"

"I've never been to Magaluf but I have a feeling I wouldn't like it." I replied scathingly.

"There are some nice beaches."

"At the opera?"

"No, at ..." Ron took another deep breath. I don't know why people had the need for meditation and deep gulps of air in my presence. "Pick you up at seven?"

"Sure." I smiled putting some distance between us on the stairs. "But, only if my boss doesn't want me to work late. I'm pretty integral to er..."

Whoops I'd inadvertently shown my ignorance again.

"To what?" He smiled wryly.

I shrugged, as though it was obvious. "Operations."

CHAPTER 18

I arranged for Ron to pick me up at the end of the road. I text to say I was nipping to the shop. In reality Mum's the ultimate curtain twitcher and I had the vibe Ron was a 'pick you up at the door' kind of guy. I knew my way to the gate. Anyway, we'd have been stuck at mine for ages whilst the olds reminisced about what it was like to be in the same class at school, how many paving stones you could easily trip over in the high street and what it was like having children my age.

Ok, it was sort of sweet he wanted to pick me up. Old fashioned, but sweet. Stephen would insist on meeting me places and had successfully avoided meeting my parents for the first year of dating. He avoided them most of our relationship too. Things were going to be different with Ron. He belonged to a different generation. He'd quite appreciate spending time with my parents. In a few years they can all go to the day centre together. Not that any of it matters because this wasn't a date. So, why had I told Mum that I might stay over with a friend in town? The shaving and exfoliating routine was to demonstrate I was, slowly coming back to me. All this preparation was just like taking an umbrella out to make sure it didn't rain.

I told Mum that I might stay over with a friend because I didn't want Dad to wait up and worry. That was all. I couldn't bear the third degree either when Mum found out it was the same 'gentleman friend' as before. Hopefully Ron wasn't a serial killer. I hadn't told a close friend where I was going. Janice would just love it if I was murdered in any of the ways I'd taken odds she would be on her first 'internet date'. That was a fun day at work. The computers were down. I spilt coffee on something called a 'server'. They'd all be relieved at work if I was bumped off... Maybe I should just text Mum.

No Jen, be reasonable. Rational. You've been out before. He's much older than you. You'd outrun him.

You wouldn't. He's much fitter than you. He's also, even with his age, like an 8 or 9. I'd be a 7 on a good day. If he was out killing young women it would definitely be models.

The age gap means I can admit Ron's devastatingly handsome. In the same way all those people were going ape about that handsome monkey on the internet a few years ago. I chuckled to myself. Clever word play, Jen. Way to stop thinking about being murdered too.

I never used to think people were out to cause me harm. At least, not until the person I trusted most did.

I had told Dad I was going to the Opera. He'd stomped around the house singing, 'Go compare,' demonstrating his up-to-the-minute referencing. I tried to imagine Ron making such unbearable Dad jokes to his daughter. I wonder if he told her where he was going tonight, or with whom. Maybe they had a strained relationship and I was a substitute. Maybe I was looking for another father figure. Although I quickly dispatched that idea when Dad appeared in the doorway with a black cape and fake moustache, both fashioned from a bin liner, as part of his 'routine'. One father was more than enough.

It's not that I was embarrassed to be seen with Ron. It's just that I didn't want to have to answer questions about it at work, or at home. That's why I'd run ahead of him on the stairs this morning and pretended not to notice when he'd arrived on our floor mid afternoon. If we'd spent all afternoon talking we'd have nothing to say to each other tonight. Not that we ever struggled for things to talk about. It was only when I mentioned the shop he'd move conversation on. He wasn't alone. People were exhausted listening to my tale of devastation. Mum, Dad, Neil, that man who came to fix the Sky TV, the Jehovah's Witnesses that came to the door that day. You would have thought they'd have been better listeners.

Maybe it was more complex for Ron. He might be confused too about what was unfolding between us. No one liked hearing the ex-files, particularly if you think you might be the one picking up the emotional tab for it all. Also, I did have 'a tendency to go on about how my life was over before it really started'. I missed Neil. He was so wise. If I was still going to the Job Centre I could have asked all his advice on this. He'd have given it then hastily add, 'you know this isn't the kind of personal advisor I'm supposed to be'. Still, Neil knew I couldn't afford a therapist and it was in his best interests to keep me as mentally stable as possible for the dwindling job market.

"Gorgeous as ever." Ron kissed me on the cheek.

So we had become friends who welcome each other with a kiss. Lovely, platonic, friendly kisses. *Damn.* I mean, good.

I never understood what it meant to have an 'infectious smile'. I thought it was a euphemism for cold sores and the spread of the herpes virus but when Ron smiled I could feel the muscles in my face involuntarily mirror his. I loved it when he smiled. I hated it too. I knew, whatever I told myself there was or wasn't between us, I was done for.

"You're not supposed to make personal comments to people at work." They had made me do two HR modules about it.

"We're not at work."

"But we're connected through work." I sighed. "It's like you haven't even read the handbook."

He tensed. As though perhaps our meeting here tonight was inappropriate.

"They wrote two new sections just for me."

I felt quite proud of that.

It seemed to make Ron more anxious.

"You look very smart." I stroked the breast pocket of his pin stripe suit. Any excuse to touch him. No, it was just a nice suit.

"No dress down Friday tonight." He tried to be flippant but I felt his chest tense.

It wasn't that nice a suit.

I wondered what Ron wore to hang around the house. No fleecy leopard print onesie for him. I repressed a smile thinking of Ron going to bed in three piece flannel pyjamas. Why was I thinking about what he would wear in bed? And what he might not?

My cheeks flushed.

Breathe.

"Are you ok?" Ron brushed his hand against my face.

"Just a bit hot." I rolled down the window.

Calm down Jen. You're in a Volvo. This is a Dad car. It's a Granddad's car. There was a child's seat hastily thrown into the boot. I hadn't even had children and Ron was on the next generation. He wouldn't want to do parenthood all over again and I couldn't be a grandmother. *Jen, you're spiralling. There was a weird moment at the weekend but the moment has passed. You understand each other. That's all.*

"Are you sure you're ok? You're a bit quiet." Ron looked concerned.

I didn't want the distance back, for it to feel as though he was drifting away. "Just thinking."

"Thank goodness! I thought that noise was coming from the engine."

See, a Dad joke. A potent reminder of where we all stood.

"I'm glad you didn't bring the pox ridden car. Talking of midlife crises. " Not that we had been. "What's this play all about? I heard operas aren't even in English and there's some kind of subtitle situation for the Latin. Am I going to have to read?"

"Why do you do that?" He stared fixedly at the road ahead.

"Do what?"

"Pretend you're just some dumb bimbo when, clearly, you're not."

"You think this is an act?" I had to wear my fool badge with pride to negate some of its power.

"You had your own business."

"Yeah, ask me how that's going. Then, when your done with that ask me about my boyfriend, sorry, ex-boyfriend. Well, I suppose it's complicated."

"The past few months doesn't define your whole existence."

What did he know? Sitting there, staring blankly ahead. Hands at the ten and two position. Textbook.

The bank sure as hell disagreed that my entire existence could not be reduced to the events of the past few months. They owned my existence now and in all perpetuity.

Ron drove like my Dad. All cautious and sensible. Stupid car. Stupid opera.

Stephen used to drive like a road runner on speed; pulling out too quickly, too impulsively at junctions. Parking illegally to go and buy chewing gum. Just some of the many ways he demonstrated he was unhinged. I'd lost count of the number of parking fines I'd paid because they were sitting in a drawer causing me anxiety. He'd been draining money off me for years.

"Why a Bookshop?" Ron broke into my reflections.

"Why... whatever it is you do?" Because you already told me, it was daddy's idea and you just fell into it.

Silence.

That had been rude. It wasn't his fault. He was only trying to... Well, I hadn't worked out what his game was and it was inconceivable he didn't have one.

"I'm not sure." I wanted to be honest. It was important to be honest. Like, 'if you're not going to give me money for my stupid book I'm going to take it anyway'. I sometimes wonder what would have happened if I'd just said yes.

Ron's question was reasonable. Why a Bookshop? It had been my dream. I had cried for weeks. I hadn't slept in months and yet, I couldn't remember why.

That was silly. Think about it.

"I like books." The words fell out of my mouth with such a lack of conviction I surprised myself.

It should have been more passionate. I should have been able to talk for hours about the why. I liked flamingos, but I was hardly going to upend my whole life and open a sanctuary in... wherever flamingos are from. I'd Google it later.

CHAPTER 19

I never imagined I'd be someone to tolerate opera. The TV commercials advertising crap we don't need would have us believe it's just a load of people screeching. If anything, I thought Dad's impromptu 'Go Compare' performance was going to the theatrical highlight of the night. Perhaps that's why I was enjoying it; I had such low expectations. There's a lesson for life in there.

I'd been put off trying anything new after my thirtieth birthday and the ballet. I hated it. Stephen complained bitterly about the cost of the tickets, the drinks and without a touch of irony, 'there's too much dancing'. Maybe it wasn't the ballet I was disappointed in that evening.

It didn't matter that I didn't speak Italian. I don't know why I quipped that it was in Latin. I didn't always need to read the subtitles either. The music and the performance communicated more than the words ever could. A group of artists and philosophers living in destitution, suffering for their art, opposing the expectation (and the sensible solution) to just go get a 'proper job.' It was going to be inspirational. A reminder that in order to get to the top of our game we have to endure the bottom. I was there. That was me. Sure, I didn't have Mimi's hacking cough...

The cough was getting worse. That'd be the poverty. Any minute one of this talented lot would catch a break. There'd be a remarkable turn around and it would all be ok.

Any minute now.

...I don't like where this is going.

"Mimi's going to be ok, right?" I whispered. My voice breaking with emotion.

Ron reached over and calmly took my hand. I felt a flash of excitement. It almost distracted me from the desperate scene relentlessly unfolding on the stage. A persistent march of events I was powerless to stop. I held Ron's hand tighter.

I couldn't speak when they brought the curtain down. I only noticed I was crying when Ron handed me a tissue.

It was just a stupid play. Just because Mimi died in destitution didn't mean I was going to. Mimi had love. I didn't even have that. I mean, it's not that I envied her the TB. I was only crying because this was life's little reminder it didn't allow for happy endings. This wasn't made by Walt Disney and the 'it'll be ok in the end brigade'. This was made by, I don't know, someone who has the same name as a mushroom. See! Ron was right. I did it again. Humour to mask the darkness and the reality that no matter how crappy it all is now, it's only going to get worse.

"It's very moving." Ron kissed my hand gently. I was suddenly confused as to whether we were still talking about the opera.

"The person who ditched you and this had the right idea." I had to move us back onto safer ground. I had to build up the defence wall he kept pointing at and knocking down. "Aren't you supposed to be cheering me up? I haven't experienced this kind of emotional trauma since the dog died."

Ron opened his mouth to speak.

"Jen!" A shriek broke the silence.

"Carol!" They said it wasn't over until the fat lady sung. Not that Carol was fat. She wasn't only a 'self-confessed foodie' but a 'gym bunny'. I hated her. My list of enemies was increasing by the day and for ever more minor infractions. Come the revolution, and trust me I'd been planning one, there'd be a number of people first up against the wall. I'd need the Great Wall of China at this rate. Maybe I'd warm to a few of them on the flight over. Maybe I'd get some perspective that the woman who'd bought my designer sunglasses when the shop and its contents were sold off piece by piece wasn't the one dimensional vulture I'd imagined. Bitch. I couldn't even afford eye cream now. I'd look older than Ron soon. I hope those glasses gave her scurvy and scrofula. Whatever that was.

"I thought that was you!" Carol pushed her way through a row of people behind us. "Alice!" She hollered. "It is Jen!"

I felt like the whole world turned to look.

"Mr. Smith." A man appeared behind Ron and tapped him gently on the shoulder. We were having a moment. Sure, I was trying to move on from the moment but, this was feeling like an ambush. Ron let go of my hand and jumped up like a scalded cat. Or the lightly wet cat that Neil had spilled his squash on at the Job Centre. Lucky slightly perturbed cat, that Neil didn't have a grown up hot drink.

Ron dashed to the end of the row to speak to the man leaving me alone, with Carol.

"I said that was you sitting a few rows in front of us but as Alice said, where would Jen get the money for opera? And, how could she possibly get better seats than us?" Carol laughed.

"Alice didn't think this would be your kind of thing." The latter comment echoed Carol's own perspective. Carol often placed her words in Alice's mouth.

Back to reality with a bump. "I'm here with a friend." I struggled to get the word out, 'friend'.

Ron had instantly abandoned me when he'd encountered someone from his real life. I shouldn't be angry. I was the one who didn't want the world to know but, had he stuck around for this, I would have introduced him.

I lowered my voice. I hoped Carol would match my level. *Inside voice, Carol. Inside voice.*

Carol needed the world to notice her. Even as a child. She always felt overbearing. In the stillness and beauty that had been tonight her presence felt completely inappropriate but, it wasn't. Carol was a reminder of the life that existed outside of this theatre; as that suited man was for Ron. Two worlds colliding. We didn't exist in a vacuum. We couldn't pretend anymore.

I could see Carol's eyes searching the room, catching sight of Ron. He smiled awkwardly in my direction. I felt rebuked. Thrown aside when one of his posh business contacts neared. His dirty little secret that couldn't be introduced. Not in polite society. The horror I glimpsed on his face answered any questions about whether Ron had told his daughter he was with me. Ron hadn't told anyone.

"Sorry." He mouthed as the suited man gesticulated, laughed and slapped him on the back.

They could be laughing about you.

I looked away.

"Him!" Carol hollered. "You're either much smarter than we've given you credit for or a hell of lot more stupid."

CHAPTER 20

"Sorry I didn't introduce you." Ron caught up with me in the hallway and handed me a glass of wine.

"I couldn't remember that man's name." A pathetic excuse for why he'd run off.

I had been leaving. Ron wouldn't have to be embarrassed by my presence any longer. One thing made me pause.

That man looked familiar. I'd been so preoccupied hating Carol, and resenting Ron, it had taken me some time to realise.

"Who was he?" Maybe he worked with us. By Monday the whole office would know. 'Sleeping her way to the top', that's what they'd think. I wasn't getting sex or promotion out of this.

"Was that the infamous Carol?" Ron deflected.

"She seemed to recognise you." It sounded like an accusation. It felt like it too.

"Lots of people do."

"I didn't and I work for you."

The quizzical look appeared on his face again. "I asked you why the book store. I didn't ask you why Smiths."

"I wanted to work in mergers and acquisitions." I quipped. "Those were my first words."

His face darkened again.

"What have I said now?" I felt his exasperation.

"It's nothing." He tried to hand me the drink again. "Sorry, tonight shouldn't have been about work. I was just asking why Smiths?"

Smiths. As though the place was unconnected to him.

"Isn't the bigger question why you gave me a job? Why you keep letting me work there?" Each and every error Ron had found in our department belonged to me.

"I'm not involved in decisions at that level."

His statement may have tried to sound dismissive of the question rather than me.

Ron tried to usher me to a chair. I wasn't going to sit down and have a drink. I was annoyed and aware how ridiculous this whole thing was. I was going home. Well, back to my parents and that sodding princess bed.

"What are mergers and acquisitions anyway?" I heard the continued frustration in my voice.

"Do you really want me to tell you?" His voice wounded. As though I was the one ruining the evening.

"Why didn't you introduce me?" I hated that I sounded so weak. I knew why Ron didn't introduce me. I wasn't important.

"Lots of people recognise me. I don't always remember them. He was very dull man, Jen. You weren't missing much."

"You told me you had a thing for faces." Hardly ever in the shop he said. Just a thing for faces he said.

Didn't remember the Florentine's though. Or the signed copy of the *Hitchhiker's Guide to the Galaxy* that sat in a display box next to the cash register. I told everyone about that book. *Everyone*.

"Only pretty ones." He tried to smooth out the discomfort. "I'm terrible with names. You said yours was Bob, didn't you?"

I wasn't going to be cajoled. There was something in Carol's face. Recognition and horror.

"So, it wasn't that you were embarrassed?"

"Embarrassed?"

"To be seen with me." I was pathetic. I really had just said that out loud. This was a new low. I put the glass down on the ledge and made to leave. "I'll see you around."

Ron gently took hold of my hand. "You can't really think that?" He looked hurt, really hurt.

Good.

Only, his pain made this worse, not better.

What could he say? What could I say? This had moved from what to what? Maybe it hadn't shifted at all. Maybe this was all in my head. We could be tactile. It was easy to hug, kiss and hold hands because this wasn't a relationship. We'd never have a relationship.

We'd never be equals. Ron had shed loads of cash and I was one step away from being homeless.

"Why Smiths?" He asked again.

Even though it was his company that seemed to be causing the tension.

"Why not?" I shrugged. Not wanting to admit the truth.

Ron looked disappointed.

"Neil needed a win." I rushed the words.

"Neil?"

"He was assigned my case at the Job Centre and his life was going rapidly down the drain." Maybe his life was worse than mine.

"I arrived early for my appointment one day."

Ron would know that was not my pattern.

"No one knew that I was there." Don't say in Jen. He has little respect for you as it is.

Ron's gentle eyes encouraged me to continue.

"I overheard a few of his colleagues bitching about me. They said I had worked for myself because no one else would employ me. You can go meet them if you like. Help list all of my failings."

He ignored the provocation. "So you took the job to prove them wrong?"

"I took the job because Neil defended me." It sounded so ridiculous but Ron had asked for the truth.

"I made that man's life a living hell and he defended me. When he thought I would never even know. I might not know much, Ron but, I know that is the mark of a true friend. Neil needed a win and I needed a job. I took the one at your company because it was the first I was offered."

"That's it?" It felt as though he was both impressed and underwhelmed by the story.

"That's it."

"Thank you for telling me that." Relief and sincerity in his tone.

Maybe Ron thought the bust Bookshop was a cover and I was planning a hostile takeover at Smiths. It sounded a lot less fun now I knew the true terminology. I initially thought Dave had said Smiths had undertaken a 'hostage take over' and that felt like some kind of revolution.

Ron pulled me closer. "Jen, you're smart, funny and caring. Please don't think I was hiding you. I was protecting you. That man, like many of the others in my work life, is none of those things. You wouldn't have wanted to meet him."

"How did you know what he was like if you don't remember him."

Ron sighed. "It's what they're all like."

"He looked familiar." I tried to reach into the recesses of my memory. I'd seen that snake before. You see, somehow I knew he was a snake.

"I think they're cloning them somewhere." Ron whispered conspiratorially, looking around at the other cardboard cut outs passing for people.

I could feel his breath on my face. Standing so close felt intimate. It felt right. Ron was making me forget about the irritating man and the niggling feeling that not only did I recognise him but, I hated him too. What the hell, I hated everyone.

"I've had a wonderful evening." Ron whispered and suddenly the rest of the world was gone.

I wanted to ask him what he would have said if he had introduced me. I wanted to ask him what this was. Instead I smiled, complicit with the denial of anything else but this moment.

"I'm lucky you have all these unreliable friends who keep letting you down."

He leaned in even closer. Our lips almost touched. "I'm lucky to have you."

The atmosphere had shifted again to become, something else.

CHAPTER 21

Events had taken a rather strange turn after the opera. Ron and I had stayed at the bar. The atmosphere easier and, somehow, also more intense. The cloned man and all the other doppelgangers had long since gone on to the next trendy place to be. I can't imagine they'd enjoyed the opera. I'm not even sure they understood it. Human emotion would not compute. The opera was just the place to be seen.

Ron casually stretched his arm across the back of my chair. "I saw how moved you were."

"Displaced grief. I couldn't give a crap that Lulu kicked the bucket."

"And again," he leaned in closer. "The pretence you don't know or care what's going on around you."

"You've got me sussed. But, who are you?" I leaned in closer too, "because in the office I hear them call you Diablo."

Ron jumped up from his chair as though he'd been electrocuted.

"Only because that's what I'm telling people. Are you ok?" I'd hit a nerve. The atmosphere between changed. Playful Ron had gone.

"What are you reacting to?" The image of the graffitied glass on his shiny new building flashed again into my mind.

"Wanker. That's you?" The word scrawled for the world to see. "Who was calling you a wanker? Why?"

"I have to go." Ron cleared his throat again.

"You did that earlier." A nervous tic from the personification of calm. "You made the same noise when you spoke about my shop."

"It's the dry air."

It wasn't. It was some kind of tell. "You're lying."

"Don't be ridiculous." The same silly little noise and a lack of conviction to his tone.

"I'm being ridiculous?" My raised voice attracted the attention of the people at the next table.

'Him?' Carol had shrieked.

"Let me get you a taxi." Ron rushed.

The shift in atmosphere was almost comic.

"Literally one of the first things I said to you when we met was this place is Hell. It's your business. You had to realise that made you the Devil." I had wanted the words to sound light and jovial but they sounded like a further accusation.

Ron gestured for the bar tender to collect our bill. "Can you get my companion a taxi, please?" There was a sudden urgency and formality in his tone.

128

"You're companion?" I sneered. "Is that what we are? Don't worry," I grabbed my coat. "I can take care of myself. I don't need a taxi."

I couldn't bloody afford one either.

I looked around the bar pointedly. "See another of your important colleagues?"

I didn't give him time to answer. I was done with games. I'd allowed myself to believe Ron was protecting me from dull people. I had no choice now to accept there was something darker at play.

"Jen!" Ron raced after me. "Please, don't leave things like this." There was an appeal in his voice but something else too. Ron appeared to both want me to leave and also to stay. "Let me get you a taxi."

"No thanks." I continued walking. "Go and join your friends."

They could talk about spreadsheets and numbers. They could forget about human emotions and feelings.

"It's not like that." He offered no other explanation.

"You can't be walking around town at this time of night." Ron tried to reason.

"It's fine. I'm wearing neutral gang colours."

I'd walked around town this time of night a thousand times before but, always with Stephen. I suddenly felt older, wiser and much more vulnerable. I hated that I felt so grown-up and responsible when I least wanted to.

Ron followed me out into the street. He quickly hailed a taxi. "Get in." He opened the door. It was perhaps intended to feel like an invitation rather than a command.

"It's out of hours, Mr. Smith. You can't boss me around now." I slammed the taxi door and stormed off down the street.

"WANKER!" The taxi driver called after Ron.

Couldn't agree more mate. "That's a popular opinion."

"Just let a taxi take you home. That's all I meant." Ron's voice was gentler now. As though trying to cajole an unreasonable child.

He'd been charming and lovely, then distant and now back. Fool me once shame on you. Fool me twice and, well I'd have to sell some vital organs on the dark web if another shady boyfriend did me over. Not that he was my boyfriend. Not that he was anything. *Keep saying it Jen. Say it until you believe it.*

"Jen, please."

I wanted him to rest his head against mine. I wanted to feel like the world was just drifting away, but that was gone. So too was the man I was falling for.

No, not falling for, becoming friends with. It didn't matter what was happening between us. I would never feel the same about him. I would never trust him again. *Silly, silly Jen. You weren't supposed to let this happen again.*

"Please, just go home in the taxi. So I know that you're safe."

"Why?" I snapped, my voice full of anger and hatred. "Planning on having me killed?"

The words shocked us both.

I stopped. "Sorry."

You can't joke about death with people who have lost someone they loved.

"I'm just so tired." I felt the words in my soul. At least, what was left of it. "I'm tired of all the games. I'm tired of being made to feel like an inconvenience."

"That is not what I intended." Ron's face plagued with regret. "Jen, you have to know this is complicated."

"No, Ron. I don't even know what *this* is." There was exasperation in my tone now too.

"Please, just let me go home. Let me do things my way." So much of my life was under other people's control.

"I'm so sorry." Ron rested his head against mine.

Too late. Too, too late.

"I'm sorry," he whispered. "Jen, you have to know how I feel about you. This wasn't supposed to happen. I wasn't supposed to fall in love with you."

CHAPTER 22

"Morning," Ron whispered in my ear.

The first thing I felt was his arm and body cocooned around me. A ridiculous rom-com sleeping position that I had convinced myself never happened in the real world.

"Morning." I rolled over and kissed him. Thinking only too late about morning breath, about how unattractive I always looked with bed hair and last night's make-up staining his pillows.

I knew that Ron didn't love me. He would be infatuated with me. I could be initially intriguing. The feeling would pass soon and I would have my heart broken all over again. Only, in this moment, in this place, none of that seemed to matter.

Perhaps I could convince myself that the success of a relationship wasn't longevity. Success could come from the things we had learnt along the way.

Perhaps there wasn't ever a 'one'. Maybe there was no such thing as Mr. Right. Only, Mr. here-right-now.

Ron could be 'the one' in that he was the person I needed for this new phase of my life.

There was a comfortable silence between us.

"What are you thinking about?" He stroked the side of my face.

I should have been thinking about how much I wanted to run away and how quickly I could do it. I should have been thinking a million conflicting thoughts. In a world that usually consumed by noise, I had the rare gift of silence.

"Nothing." A new-found calm. No anxiety. No self-doubt. Only contentment.

I mean, I suppose its contentment. It's such an unfamiliar feeling I didn't have the words to understand it, let alone articulate it to another.

"You can be completely honest." Ron looked deep into my soul. Honesty was rarely something people asked for from me. "I won't be overly offended if it's something random."

"Like what?" I feigned protest.

Ron laughed. "I don't know. Like, do birds have ears?"

He knew me too well.

"Do they?" I was suddenly perplexed by the question.

"No regrets?" The strong, confident, self-assured man lay naked and vulnerable.

"Not about this." I held him closer. "You?"

He shook his head because in this flat, in this moment, the world felt very far away.

CHAPTER 23

My mobile phone buzzed into action as I headed down the street into work. Carol. No way Carol. Not today. I was on a high and not about to let her burst my bubble. Not today, or any other day in fact. This was my rebirth. A new me. A more positive me. This new me knew I positively did not want to speak to Carol. Ever.

Last night was amazing. Beyond amazing. The first time with a guy, not that I had a vast amount of experience, was always an awkward fumble. When it was over I usually felt a sense of relief; either that it was out of the way or it was so dreadful I'd never have to see him again. I'd never slept with someone and felt such a connection. It was so tender. So right. My stomach flipped again thinking of being in Ron's arms. Deeply entwined yet, still feeling it wasn't enough. Wanting more.

'I wasn't supposed to fall in love with you.' The vulnerability in Ron's words echoed in my ears. It had made me happy to hear him say it. Happy last night to live in that lie.

Ron and I had known each other such a short space of time. I didn't believe in love at first sight. As magical as our connection had been it wasn't enough to shift my world view. I hadn't allowed myself to think about my feelings for Ron. I knew already they were too deep. Already I was on the heartbreak highway and this loss could be more devastating than the last.

My face flushed as I floated in early to the office. People would see I was different. I'd have to explain the dumb smile that refused to leave my face. Maybe I could convince everyone it was just a concussion. Or, I'd finally resorted to drugs. No, legal highs. Much trendier.

'Maybe we're in different places.' I ventured as we lay together. Children had always been part of the plan with Stephen but, look what happens to plans.

I hadn't wanted to ask. I hadn't wanted to be that person, 'would you want more kids?'

I tried to sound relaxed, as though it was merely a passing thought. The atmosphere had been so light-hearted I dreaded a flippant response like, 'I couldn't eat a whole one'. Ron kissed my neck, 'who knows what the future could bring. I never imagined you'. I flushed with relief, suddenly aware I'd been holding my breath.

'You need to know one thing.' Ron held me close. 'Whatever happens from here on in, I love you. I want a future with you'. His face darkened. 'It might not be easy and, you may change your mind.'

I protested too quickly, 'I won't'. I wanted to say that I loved him. That I trusted him too. I wanted to tell Ron that he'd helped heal my brokenness as he'd told me I'd healed his but, I couldn't. So instead, I pulled him closer and showed him again how much he meant to me.

"Afternoon." David barked as he looked at his watch. He ploughed on, confused. It was so impossible I should be on time. That's the cataclysmic shift that had taken place in the world. I had David doubting Mickey Mouse.

I hadn't wanted to leave Ron's bed. We'd kissed. We'd showered together. We'd made love again.

Argh! I had just said, 'made love'. I hated my smug self.

"You're lucky Mr. Smith has a meeting in town."

Who did he think dropped me at the end of the road? Ron's going to be late for that meeting. Elated and late.

My phone buzzed again. Mum. I'd call her back. David was still giving me the evil eye and I didn't want to push it too much. Not now I had decided life had meaning again and realised everything did indeed happen for a reason. It really was all going to be ok. No, it was going to be fabulous.

'Fall in love with you'. The words span around, echoing in my head. I saw that look of intensity scorched across his face. Wanting to do the right thing but pleasuring me with the wrong. Ron wanted a future together and it could be easy. He was just a little older.

Ron nuzzled my neck, electrifying my body with his touch, 'I never thought I could be this happy. There's a lot we need to get past but, I promise you, it's all just footnotes.'

I resisted telling him I'd never understood footnotes. Don't even read them. There's no point in the small print.

I could smell his aftershave on me.

Love.

I hadn't said it. I couldn't. I had to be sure of him. I had to be sure of me. Yet, when I woke up in Ron's arms I knew and understood; I was exactly where I needed to be.

I'd call Mum in twenty minutes. She'd worry if I didn't. I'd busy myself for bit. David and Janice seemed to find it more annoying I was actually early.

Twenty minutes then I would be my ever helpful self and ask if anyone would like a coffee. I'd call Mum then. Of course, I had to send her a quick text, 'broccoli'. It means, 'I can't talk right now but I've used our code word so you know it's me. I definitely haven't been murdered.' She'd probably just think some psycho had tortured it out of me. Mum watched way too many true crime documentaries. I'm a bit worried she's planning to off Dad.

Janice glared at me, full of suspicion. "What are you so bloody happy about?"

CHAPTER 24

Being happy annoyed more people than my usual sullen self. What a topsy turvy world we live in. They should all find love like Ron and I. Love can conquer all. Except, as it seems, wild camping. The weekend with what's-his-face had not gone well for Janice.

"That's the thing with these rescue sites."

"It's internet dating." She protested.

"Sure, you read all their sad wee biographies about what a hard life they've had but you get them home and they bite you and crap on the carpet."

"It was that one time." Janice snapped.

"What happened that one time?" David seemed shocked into interest in Janice's sexscapades.

I wasn't.

"Are you just letting that one pass?" David directed his irritation towards me. I often thought he used me to unearth all the dark recesses of Janice's life.

"I have other more important things on my mind. "I nodded to the pile of papers on my desk and wondered if they were the same ones from two weeks ago. Well, a small part of my brain wondered. The majority was thinking about Ron.

I tried not to think about how sombre he'd looked this morning. Or his overreaction when I joked he might be the devil. I pushed out of my head the taxi driver had called him a wanker. The same word someone kept scrawling across the front of his building. I didn't let myself think about the sad look in his eyes or the dreadful feeling I was about to find out something I didn't want to know.

Like what? This is so you, Jen. Self-sabotage. That's what the article would have called it. The same thing your sixth year Chemistry teacher accused you of.

Maybe Ron had remarried. Maybe the child's seat was for a little person he hadn't told me about. Not a grandchild. Maybe he was still in love with his wife. Perhaps Ron felt he was betraying her as, on some level, I felt I'd betrayed Stephen. My mind was a whirl of a thousand competing thoughts all wanting to be heard and one other. A thought I'd locked away in the darkest corners of my psyche because not even I wanted to see it. Carol's face when she saw Ron. I wondered whether it was fame or infamy I had read there. I wondered too why Carol was calling.

Stop it. The past is dripping into the present and destroying the future. You've no reason to doubt Ron.

You'd no reason to doubt Stephen.

This was different. I was different.

139

Only, why did the company have an image problem? Why did our building keep getting defaced?

Mum's right. I can't allow myself to be happy. Maybe I'm only happy when I have a problem. Or, when clinging desperately to something I didn't want.

Like Stephen. Like the shop.

No, I'd wanted them both. Hadn't I?

This is ridiculous! I'd had a glorious night. Why couldn't I just accept that? I took a deep breath and remembered the joy of truly being in the moment. At no point last night, or this morning, had I wanted to be anywhere else; any time else. There was no looking back or forward. It was perfect.

I drew myself back to the present where, added bonus, my good mood was increasing Janice's usual level of frustration. She kept finding ever more pointless and pressing tasks for me to complete to try and break my new found spirit. It was almost lunch time before I eventually escaped for coffee. I snuck my mobile phone from the desk. Careful to escape the overbearing watchful eye of the all-seeing Janice. She had more of an omnipresent feel now she seemed to be wearing less of the fake eyelashes.

"You have nice eyes, Janice." I offered up a sincere compliment as I fled from the room.

"Fuck off."

She was so defensive about everything.

'Jen, can you meet me for lunch? There's something I want to discuss. Ron x'

He used punctuation in texts. Of course he did.

"What was that?" Janice looked at the phone desperately. "Are you on a dating app?"

"Sure, I am. My parent's house is nice but I think what would really cheery it up is a giant turd in the corner."

"You live in your parent's house?" David joined the conversation again.

I had told these people so little of my real life.

"They live with me." I felt bad about the lie. "I'm really only working here to help you guys out."

"Thanks." His voice lacked conviction.

I looked again at the message from Ron on my phone.

'Discuss'. My heart sank. 'Discuss' was never good. There had been a lot of 'discussions' with Neil at the Job Centre, then his line manager.

I'd clicked on the message. Ron would know I'd read it. Blooming technology. Maybe he didn't know how to work his phone. Dad frequently sends me pictures of his ear.

The phone buzzed again.

"Sorry Mum." I rushed to answer as I ran down the stairs to the side exit I shouldn't be using.

"It's been a manic day. I was just about to call you back." I wondered whether I should tell her about Ron. Now love had been mentioned and a future hung in the air.

"The Police arrested Stephen." She rushed.

Silence.

"Did you hear me?" Her concerned disembodied voice echoed from my phone.

I don't know.

"The Police have arrested Stephen." She repeated.

The street was beginning to spin. I grabbed onto a nearby wall. Unfortunately, it was one of the cardboard cut-out people; easy to mistake for inanimate objects.

"Hey!" The stranger swiped my hand away.

"They picked him up in Brighton. He was using his bank card to buy a train ticket at the station."

Idiot.

Hang on. "Why was he using his card if he had all my money?"

Oh. Of course. Gone. All of it.

I was finding it hard to breath. Until now I had a glimmer of hope that even if Stephen never returned the money might.

"His Mum had a stroke. Just a little one but..." Her voice trailed off.

"But, Margaret's ok?"

"I think so." Mum was apprehensive in her response. As though I had missed the point of what she was telling me. Then, I realised. Someone had known how to contact him.

"The Police wanted to come to your work and update you but, I wouldn't allow it. I said you'd be embarrassed."

I would have told David and Janice I was undercover. That would have made David regret talking at us for forty minutes last week about some dodgy stick he had plugged into his TV to hack the streaming services.

I was beyond embarrassed about any of this.

Mum continued to speak but her words were just background noise.

I felt sick.

Stephen had been arrested. The man I had known and loved for seven years was being questioned by the Police for a crime he'd committed. A crime against me.

"Are you ok?" I could hear panic in Mum's voice. "I told your Dad we should wait until you came home but, I didn't want you hearing it from anyone else."

"It wasn't just a mistake then?" The words came out so hollow.

"No, love." Mum spoke gently. "Stephen knew what he was doing when he took the money. I think he understands too that it was wrong."

Did he? Or was that just the best defence for his actions.

"It's just, a bit of a shock." I wheezed. Trying to find my breath.

"Come home. Take a half day, love. I'm sure they'll understand."

They couldn't. I hadn't told either David or Janice.

I wanted to be here, with Ron. I trusted him. I had always trusted him. Stephen had taken so much from me. I wasn't going to let him take this.

"His story backs up what you told the Police and the Bank."

143

They had thought I was planning to join Stephen in the Costa del Crime or, sunny Brighton as it seems.

"Doesn't he have a cousin there?" There was a vague memory of some connection forming.

"An ex-girlfriend." She whispered. As though that was the biggest betrayal of all.

"The insurance will pay out now." Mum was close to tears. "It's over, love."

It didn't feel over.

I tried to break it down into smaller, more digestible chunks.

Stephen was back.

The debt would be gone.

Until I could see that in my back account I wouldn't allow myself to believe it. Until I had my own place, until I knew what it was I was supposed to be doing with my life, it would never be over.

That was silly. I knew what I was meant to be doing. The Bookshop. I'd get that back. The insurance would have to pay for loss of earnings, emotional trauma and anything else my lawyer threw at them. I could have it all back. Only, I didn't want it.

Calm down, Jen. You're in shock. This isn't the time to be making decisions. You can have it all back. That was the dream. Wasn't it?

"Love." Mum paused. "There's something else."

CHAPTER 25

She hadn't understood. Mum was at that age. That's all. And, Carol being Carol of course; stirring up crap again.

So why had I come here, to her, and not to him? Ron could have cleared up this misunderstanding in a minute. I would have looked into those grey eyes and all the doubts would have washed away.

That was why.

I had to be presented with the cold hard facts before the all-consuming wave of emotion. I'd let him talk me round. I wanted to believe the lie.

"What did you tell my Mum?"

Carol shuffled uncomfortably in her chair. She had a 'pressing appointment' but months of destitution had taught me I wasn't above making a scene.

"I tried to call you." Carol accused. As though it was my fault she'd been spitting poison in Mum's ear.

"You're not supposed to worry her." I spoke defensively of the woman I had almost broken with worry over the past six months.

"I wasn't trying to *worry* her." Carol defended. As though the lies she had spread about Ron were supposed to be helpful.

"I thought you knew but, Alice said." She hesitated. "How could you have known?" Carol summarised the discussion. Now was not the time to let me know she and her wife thought I was 'dim witted' (Carol's words, not mine). Terminology aside the Stepford wives must have had a point. I'd had two disastrous boyfriends. One right after the other.

"What did you say to Mum?" I had to hear it again from the source. The full ridiculousness of it all needed to tumble from her lips.

Only... I don't know. Maybe... Maybe something about it had made sense too. Like an optical illusion that finally had its mystery revealed.

Carol offered me a drink. She was at that executive level when it was customary to have a bottle of alcohol tucked away in a drawer. When Neil did it, it was a disciplinary matter and he had a problem. Here, offering your broken cousin a shot of neat whisky just before lunch was fine. It's all about context. That's what Mum's revelation was missing; context.

How could context make this any less damning?

"Your Mum said she hasn't seen you this happy in years. Jen, I saw that too. Whatever I say next there is a

146

connection between you." Carol poured herself a large drink and knocked it back with such precision I began to wonder if she did have a problem. I made a mental note to ask her about it later then tried to scrub it. Carol wasn't my concern.

"What did you say?"

I didn't want to hear how the world could see what we felt. I wanted to hear the jumble of words that had fallen through the phone. I needed to process it; understand it.

Carol twisted her hair awkwardly in her hand. She'd done that for years. It was her 'tell'. Carol was rattled.

Her tell. I thought of Ron's anxious cough. I thought of the contextual nature of his dry throat; whenever the Bookshop was mentioned.

"Come on, Carol. We don't like each other but I've always thought there's a grudging respect between us."

"You don't like me?" Carol's voice indicated that was a revelation. As though her entire successful life hadn't been pitted against the wayward cousin's ridiculous existence.

"It's a figure of speech." I dismissed.

"Stephen didn't like me." Carol corrected.

Stephen didn't like anyone.

"You and I used to get on just fine."

There was a truth to her words too. Carol and I meeting for coffee. Laughing even. More than cousins; almost sisters.

"What did you tell Mum?" My voice softened. I wondered where the distance between us had come from and how either one of us had let it happen.

"I can't think about Stephen." The pleading was evident in my tone. I couldn't think either of the life that was ending all over again.

"I only said that I was surprised to see you with Ron Smith given that," she hesitated again. Carol of the endless words seemed to be lost for them.

"You really should be talking to him about this."

I'd had a sense of foreboding this morning. 'I want to be with you, no matter what'. He knew something I didn't. I tried to tell myself it was the age gap, but there was more. He'd turned away momentarily; concealing something. He'd drawn breath to speak. Instead he smiled and kissed me, with increasing urgency, as though that would be the last time we'd lie there together.

It made sense now. Why he changed the subject whenever I had talked about the shop. Why he'd recognised me and not the Florentines.

"Carol, please. I'm asking you." The anger drained from my voice. I was surprised how calm I felt. Deep down I'd always known Ron and I would never last. Not because our relationship was based on a lie but because all relationships were. I wanted to feel thankful I had found out so early. I wanted this not to hurt.

Carol hung her head. This should have been her moment of triumph. She should be revelling in watching my world crash around my ears, again.

"I was surprised to see you with Ron Smith because he owns the bank that foreclosed on your loan, and he owns the real estate company that sold your beautiful shop to that bloody chain." There were tears in her eyes. She tried to reach out and touch me but, I couldn't let her. I couldn't be consoled.

"You're wrong."

She wasn't.

"Maybe he doesn't know either. It's a huge company. Whatever the truth of all of this is Jen, he seemed genuinely fond of you."

"Not fond enough to introduce me to..." Oh no. The little black box in my brain flew open revealing what I didn't want to see. I remembered. The sleaze bag who approached him at the opera was the Bank Manager. The snide little creep I'd spoken to earlier today. He'd apologised for all the 'inconvenience' when three months previously, as a fully paid up member of the 'there's no smoke without fire and hangings too good for them brigade', he'd wanted me charged with fraud.

Ron knew.

"Give him a chance to explain, Jen." Carol must have known I believed her. That I would have always believed her.

"I'm not pretending I understand any of this but, I've literally marched on the street so consenting adults can share their lives, their beds, with whoever they choose."

Yup, you're a bloody martyr Carol. I looked up, mustering as much hatred as I could but the compassion in her eyes caught my breath. She actually cared.

"Your Mum said she thought you were in love." Carol reached out and grasped my hand. This time I didn't have the energy to pull away.

"This must be great for you." I tried to hate her again. I tried to hate the world. I had let myself down. I had let another deceitful man into my life.

"Jen, you're like a sister to me."

All of the years I had spent hating Carol I'd never once considered she actually loved me. As much as it appears anyone could love me.

"They caught Stephen." The words no more than a whisper.

"I know." She held my hand tighter.

"He said he loved me too. He said a lot of things."

Only, you don't lie to the people you love. You don't leave them high and dry for another Charlatan to break their heart. *No, this was about Ron*! Not Stephen. My head was spinning.

This was about me.

CHAPTER 26

There it was in black and white. Hidden amongst the footnotes and tiny writing no one reads. 'Loan underwritten by RM Smith'.

Carol hadn't been impressed that night she'd seen us together at the opera. She'd been dumb founded. I'd shacked up with the man who had obliterated my dreams after the love of my life had squandered all my money. High line message; I'm a terrible judge of character.

I wandered back to the office, dazed.

"Where they hell have you been?" David looked suddenly more concerned. "Jen, are you ok?" He ushered me towards a seat. Janice rushed over.

I'd been to the Bank. I'd insisted Clint (although that's not what I'd called him) showed me the loan contract again. He'd hesitated. He might even have contacted Ron, but now Stephen was under lock and key I had them over a barrel. Besides, it was my loan contract. It had my signature at the bottom. It was conditions I had agreed to; even if I hadn't understood them.

Carol was right.

"I can't work here anymore." I pulled my jacket from the back of the chair.

"You never really worked here before." David joked. He wanted easy Jen back. "What's happened? Have you been sacked?"

"No, but I just found out what it is we do." I looked around the bright shiny office. The presentable face of destruction. How many other people had this place annihilated? How many other lives had been broken here?

"Acquisitions." I Googled the word too late. "Where one company purchases another to expand, gain market share or, most likely, to reduce the competition. Ron has shares in three major Bookshop chains."

"He has shares in lots of things." Janice looked concerned. "Jen, why do you care about any of this?"

"Wanker." The word had appeared again on the door.

"It was a reasonable question!" Janice looked to David for back up.

"The graffiti that keeps appearing on the window downstairs. That's someone else whose business Ron has *acquired*, right?"

"Maybe." The phone rang on Dave's desk. He looked torn.

"Do you know who keeps defacing the building every morning? Why they've such commitment to it?"

A look passed between David and Janice. Perhaps there were just too many suspects.

The phone kept ringing. The tone felt urgent.

"Go ahead. Answer it." I stood up. My legs wobbled and threatened to give way. "I'm going home."

Neil would understand. At least, he would when I explained. If I continued to work for Ron it would be like Neil babysitting for his ex's hairy brother-cousin kids.

"You'll have a notice period." Janice sounded desperate. As though she actually wanted me to stay. As though she didn't want it to all end like this.

"I'm sure Mr. Smith will waive it."

"Jen," Janice put her hand on my shoulder. "What's happened? You're worrying us."

The phone kept up the incessant ring.

Dave picked up the phone and impatiently slammed it back down.

It immediately rang again.

"What?" All pretence at professionalism gone as he snapped into the mouth piece.

"Mr. Smith wants to see you." David relayed the message.

"I don't want to see him."

Ron had wanted to talk. Now I understood why.

"He seemed to be hanging about more than usual today. It could be urgent." Janice understood what it was like to have been let down so badly by a man. Janice gave her trust too easily. I understand now, that we both did.

"I know I've been a bit of a pain to work with but," I looked at David then Janice. "You two seem like fairly decent human beings. You don't want to belong here."

"Jen, it's just business." David sounded as though he didn't understand my distaste for the nature of the organisation.

"It's so much more than that."

I didn't hang around. If anyone in the office would have thought to plan a leaving party I wouldn't be invited. The celebration would be that I was gone. I didn't make any real friends. I was glad of that now. The slick, clean surfaces repulsed me.

I'd told myself this building was the future; my business was a relic of the past. This job had brought anonymity, but at what cost? Perhaps that's why they could all do such unconscionable things. They didn't have to see the consequence of it all.

I left by the side exit. I didn't want to be seen. I didn't want to be associated with any of this.

"Jen." Ron raced down the stairs. "David said you'd quit."

David was a grass. I should have asked him to give me a head start.

"Where have you been all day?" Anxiety rampant in his tone. Ron knew where I had been. He rushed to try and to hold me. I couldn't let him.

"Did you know?" The tears were cracking my voice but, I wouldn't let him see me cry. He could never see that he'd won.

Ron's face betrayed him.

"That's what I thought."

"Jen." Ron stepped forward. He tried to close the distance between us but, I wouldn't let him comfort me. I couldn't allow my defences to fall.

I'd trusted him, I'd trusted Stephen and they'd both been complicit in my downfall.

"I can explain."

He couldn't.

"What exactly has this been to you, Ron?" I folded my arms.

Hate him, Jen. Hate him.

Forget what it was like to be held by him. Forget that he was the only man who has ever made the world disappear. Forget you had ever thought this could be any kind of one.

"I should have told you from the start but you'd have hated me."

"I hate you now." I didn't but, I wanted to.

Ron looked wounded, for a dreadful second I thought he might cry.

"You said I was smart. You must have been laughing all the way to the bank with that one."

"It wasn't like that." Ron protested.

"Clint Greigson. That's his name. The clone from the opera. The smarmy git of the Bank Manager who froze all my accounts because he thought Stephen and I were in this together. Odd you didn't remember his name. He lists you as a mentor on Linked-in."

Ron looked to the floor. Ashamed, caught out or both.

"I'm so bloody stupid. Taken in again, by another con man."

"You're not stupid." Ron pleaded. "I'm the stupid one but, I'm not a con man. I should have told you my connection to all of this but, none of it was illegal."

"At least when Stephen screwed me over it was a crime. He'll have a consequence. People understood I was a victim."

"Jen, please. I never meant to hurt you."

"How did you imagine any of this would turn out, Ron?"

Silence.

"I trusted you. The devil runs off with my life and I go and fall in love with his brother."

"Love?"

"That's not what I meant. It doesn't matter now. You're not who I thought you were."

"I am. I never lied to you. I have felt more at ease with you than any other person in this world." Ron stepped in front of me, blocking the door.

"I just didn't tell you the whole truth." It sounded weak. "Jen, I've been more open and honest with you than I have with anyone in a long time."

"Then anyone in your life needs to get the hell out of it."

More honest wasn't enough.

"What was I? An unexpected bonus on an unpaid debt? What does that make me?"

"You have every right to be angry." Ron looked devastated.

"Don't stand there and lecture me on my rights." I found anger in all the pain.

"You can have it all back."

"As what? Payment for services rendered?"

Ron was right. All he and his company had done was perfectly legal. I was entitled to nothing.

"No," Ron's voice was cracking. "Please, come home with me. We can talk."

"Home." I spat the word out. "I had one of those. A beautiful flat. You should take a look at it sometime. It's yours now, isn't it?"

"Tell me how to fix this." He pleaded.

"My old shop." The tears pricked my eyes. "One of your chains is getting the premises."

"That was nothing to do with me." His tone defensive. As though he too was a victim.

"Jen," he pleaded again. "Tell me how to fix this."

"Tell me it's not true. Tell me you didn't foreclose on my loan, take my business, my flat and treat me like a criminal."

"I didn't personally do any of that." As though that exonerated him.

"But, you employed the people who did."

"It was just," his voice faded, "business."

"And the nights out? The sex? Was all that just business too?"

Silence. There was nothing left to be said.

"Don't ever contact me again." I stepped to the side, moving past him, leaving yet another sordid relationship behind.

"I tried to tell you this morning. I asked you to call me."

"Sure, sure. This is all my fault."

Smart women know who they are working for, what the company does and maybe, most importantly of all, who they are sharing their bed with.

It was his bed. It would always have been his bed. He wasn't content with owning my business and my flat. He wanted me too.

"I'm not blaming you. I accept full responsibility but."

"I'm sorry but, isn't an apology, Ron. It's an excuse."

My Mum had taught me that as a child. I finally understood it now. Perhaps that's how parenting worked. You had to watch your children make the mistakes you tried to prevent. We all had to learn our lessons the hard way.

Ron put his hand gently behind my head, making me look into those deceitful eyes I'd foolishly trusted with my heart.

"I never planned any of this. I recognised you instantly. I tried to put distance between us but, I knew from the very first moment we met that I loved you."

Impossible.

"Then I saw how broken you were and I felt sorry for you..."

"Sorry for me?" Anger. Good. I needed more of that. "Pity sex?"

"This is all coming out wrong." Ron needed time to think. Time to come up with a better defence. Perhaps get a team of lawyers involved.

"I think it's finally all coming out right."

"You're so different from anyone else I know. I connected with you in a way I've never connected with anyone."

"Well, you had me at a slight disadvantage. Everyone else knew you were a monster."

Ron looked as though he had been punched.

Good.

I'd hurt him. Not a fraction of the hurt he had caused me. So, why did his pain only cause me more?

I rested my head against his. Allowing myself for a brief second to pretend it was all going to be ok. We'd move past this. One day we would laugh with friends about how ridiculously complicated all this had become. Only, I couldn't pretend anymore. I couldn't just ignore the red flags. Stephen had inadvertently taught me a valuable life lesson. There's a vast difference between what it is you want and what it is you need.

"If you ever felt anything for me." I whispered, and looked pleadingly into his eyes. "Then, please. Never contact me again."

CHAPTER 27

"Come on, love." Mum sat down on my bed. "It's been a week. This room stinks. You stink." She tousled my hair affectionately. "At least have a bath."

"Can't." Ron's betrayal had done what nothing else the past six months could. It broke me.

I didn't have the energy to get up. I didn't have to pay the bank back anymore. The slate had more than been wiped clean. At least when I was in crippling debt I had to get up and pay my penance to the world of fat cats. No longer suspected of fraud the insurance was paying out left, right and centre. Anything I wanted.

I didn't want anything.

At least, nothing they could give.

Mum signed. "I'm sorry love, but you leave me no other choice. CAROL!"

Carol burst into the room like a tornado. "Bloody hell! You weren't exaggerating about the smell. It's like something died in here."

My hope. My ambition. My dreams.

Carol threw open the curtains and windows. "Auntie Suzie, go and run her a bath."

"And how do you plan on getting me there?" I pulled the covers over my head.

Carol yanked them off the bed. She's such a cow.

"You got your money back. You should be happy."

As though the money was all that had mattered.

"I'm elated, now leave me alone." I reached for the covers again.

"Where's the fighting spirit you always show me?" Carol challenged. "Jen, you were right what you said in my office. We admire each other."

"I didn't say I admired you." It was important Carol understood that.

"You care about people and crap no one else does."

"People care about the ice caps melting, Carol. They care about landfill."

Carol waved the concern for the demise of the planet away. "You've always been obsessed with making the world a better place. You're not going to do that rotting in bed."

The world had survived this long without me. It could manage another week.

"What Stephen did was crappy. What Ron was forced to do..."

"He's not the victim here." I broke in.

"No," Carol knelt down on the floor next to my bed and looked me straight in the eye. "But, neither are you."

162

That's not what will be said at Stephen's trial.

Carol stroked the greasy, limp hair from my face. "It's been tough but, you're back on track. It's time to fulfil your ambitions. Not the compromised version you dreamt up with Stephen and then, settled on."

"The Bookshop was my dream." Only, somewhere in the dark recesses of my mind I remembered the Bookshop hadn't been my idea.

"We've all had the fantasy that some rich man or woman is going to come and save us."

Even though it was daylight outside Carol banged on the lights. She was doing all she could to make me uncomfortable in the one place I felt safe.

"That's not how life works. We have to save ourselves. So get up and bloody do it!"

"I didn't care that he was rich." I felt the tears stream down my swollen face. I allowed myself to cry alone in the darkness.

I didn't care that he Ron was older either.

"He understood me. Not many people do." There was a vulnerability to the words that for a second, softened Carol.

"He was kind, thoughtful, funny and I loved him. I loved him more than I ever loved Stephen. I trusted him more. I thought Ron healed me. I didn't realise he was the one that broke me in the first place."

"He didn't break you." Carol sat compassionately on the edge of my bed. "A ship doesn't sink because it's

163

surrounded by water. The ship sinks because the water gets inside."

"What the buggering hell does that mean?"

"I read it on social media this morning. It felt apt. I'm not good at this."

"Failure?"

"Human emotion." Carol gestured to my crumpled body. "Bad things happen. All the time. And you can choose to be pulled under or you can steady yourself in the waves."

"That easy?"

"Of course it's not bloody easy!" Carol rolled her eyes. "I blame your parents. All those damn fairy tales and this bloody bed! Prince Charming doesn't ride in and save you. And you wouldn't want him to. Jen, we have to save ourselves. You can fix all this. You just have to face it."

"I can't." I sat up, looking pointedly around my room. "Everyone else I know is getting married, having kids, being successful. Not back living with their parents."

"Boo bloody hoo." Carol barked. "Life not quite as you planned? Join the queue, but be prepared for a wait because it's a hell of a long one." Carol sighed. "You keep focussing on what's gone wrong and not what's going right."

Carol nodded to my bedroom door. "Your life fell to crap and the first thing you did was come home. Your parents love the bones of you. They welcomed you back with unconditional love and I bet neither one of them told you what you should have done, mocked you or passed any kind of judgement. They loved you, cared for you and never once asked for anything in return. If you can't pull yourself out of this pit for you then, do it for them."

I could hear Mum breathing anxiously on the other side of the door.

"If there was a time to curl up in a ball that was six months ago." Carol grabbed my dressing gown from behind the door. "You've licked your wounds. You've paid penance. That time is finished. This doesn't break you. You can choose that here and now. This doesn't break you. Now, go and have a bloody bath."

CHAPTER 28

It should be a comfort to know that some things in life don't change. The Job Centre was one of them.

I scanned the cards for a valid career option; the computers were down again. Maybe an all female environment so I didn't fall in love with anyone. Maybe something I could see myself doing for more than the next six weeks.

"Do you think I would look good in a wimple?" I turned to the suited man next to me.

"I don't think they have Wimpy any more, love." He pointed to a card on the wall. "They're looking for a fryer at the Plaice2Be."

"No, a wimple. It's the head dress of a nun."

The man looked at me again, paused, and then backed away.

I dismissed the job at the Place2Be. I'd only just managed to get the grease out my hair from the week of 'bed rotting'.

I turned my attention back the job adverts hoping there was a career that could give my life meaning now I finally realised I couldn't find that in other people. Then it hit me. *I was wrong again!*

"Oh God." Neil sighed.

"I come in peace."

I was relieved Neil was back at work. The alopecia had settled down and he'd near as damn it kicked the nervous twitch.

"What happened this time?"

"I fell in love with the boss. Then, I realised it was his company that foreclosed on my business loan, took my shop, and my home then sold them off piece by piece to total vultures. I mean, literal strangers. Remember the cow who bought my designer sunglasses." At least I had downgraded her from bitch.

I saw that same look on his face, before 'the incident' and tried to lighten the mood. "Oh, but good news. That weird bruise on my leg is gone."

"What?" Neil tried to look disinterested. "Totally?"

I nodded enthusiastically.

Neil scanned the screen in front of him. "There's not a box to tick for any of what you just told me on the system."

For a brief moment I thought I should help the Job Centre design a new system. I was often told they didn't have a box to define my circumstances.

"Isn't there irreconcilable differences? Maybe put it went against my religious or political beliefs." Don't sleep with liars.

"I'm not here to make a claim." I didn't even need a box. "They arrested Stephen, did you hear?" I looked around conspiratorially.

"Ms. Blake, your personal circumstances." He boomed before lowering his voice. "Those incompetents found him?"

I had not been gracious about the Police in charge of my case.

"He was caught using his bank card. He was coming home. His Mum had a stroke."

"Aw, Jen." Neil's voice oozed compassion. "They knew where he was."

"Seems like it."

"I'd charge those dickheads too then." Neil looked at the small statue of the Buddha on his desk. "Karma will get them."

I'd like to say Neil was a Buddhist. Neil was an obsessive trend follower and a new meditation centre had just opened up in town.

"I want this job." I pushed the card forward. Neil had long since given up telling me not to take the cards from the boards. I'd protested it was my cut throat strategy to reduce the competition and reminded him it was all supposed to be online anyway.

"Do you want me to put the card back?"

"Nice try." Neil leaned back in his chair assuming my new helpful attitude was another ploy. "What is it this time? A job at the slaughter house? You'll make me process the application for twenty minutes and then, 'whoops, sorry. I just remembered I'm a vegan.'"

"I gave you a hard time. I'm not only going to tell you I'm sorry I'm going to show it."

An apology without a change in behaviour is just manipulation. Mum had that one on her social media motivational quotes last week. Where was this wisdom as things deteriorated with Stephen?

She would have helped if you'd told her.

I'd not only realised a lot about Stephen the past week. I'd realised a lot about myself. I had lied to the people I loved. I had lied to myself. I convinced the world around me Stephen and I were happy. I lied about our relationship so the people around me would like him.

"I wasn't coping and I shouldn't have taken that out on you." I looked back at Neil, mortified by my own honesty. I couldn't understand why I hadn't seen it before. Neil wasn't coping well either.

As I looked around the Job Centre I saw the same anxiety and despair in the faces of others. It wasn't that the people here had no aspirations. Their plans and dreams had been eroded by the harsh realities of life. A quick glance at the commuters outside confirmed my worst suspicions; there were hordes of us all living a compromised existence. Maybe the trick was knowing where to compromise.

We all had our own little personal Armageddon. Everyone got up each day and fought some kind of battle no one else knew anything about. Sure, some were bigger than others but sometimes, no matter the trial, we just didn't have the energy or the strength to face it. It's not always what we have to endure; it's often how long we have to endure it. Carol was right. I'd never tell her to her face but, we don't need someone to save us. When our world implodes sometimes all people can do is sit with us in the darkness. Then, when we're ready, walk beside us and show us the way out of the pit; a pit I'd willingly leapt into with Stephen.

"If I'm being totally honest," even I was interested in what I was going to say next. "I was frightened to make any kind of effort because then, when I failed again, at least I wasn't really trying. But, the Bookshop wasn't my dream. This is what I wanted to do."

I tapped the card. "This is the job I want. I want to make a difference."

You could find happiness in other people. You just had to be careful which ones.

"Will you help me to do this, please?"

Shocked by my sudden lack of defence mechanisms Neil was lost for words. Eventually he sighed, then smiled.

"You have made a difference." He pointed to his natty badge, 'I'm allergic to nuts'.

Boy, is he ever! I've never actually seen a person's head swell up before.

Neil looked at the card again and smiled. "This could be a pretty tough gig."

"Yeah, well. I'm no longer afraid of a challenge."

A thought suddenly occurred to me. "Hey, Neil. You think I would look good in a wimple, right?"

CHAPTER 29

"He called again, love." Mum was reluctant to speak his name. Particularly at breakfast. That could start the day off poorly.

"He wanted you to meet him in town today at one. He said you'd know where."

I wasn't going to meet him. I had nothing to say. I'd been planning on going into town but, I wasn't going to meet him. I never wanted to see him again. I was going to treat myself to something nice to wear for my interview on Tuesday and, I had to get out the house. Daytime TV had fulfilled its function by making me feel like a well-adjusted member of society. Yes, I had been unlucky but I hadn't unknowingly married my half-brother.

Being unemployed again was hard. Mum kept hanging around, taking a deep breath, as though about to say something meaningful and profound, before just asking if I wanted my four hundredth cup of tea. There were no words left for all this. Mum's eyes betrayed a million questions she knew I didn't have the answers to. Even Dad had wandered in from the garage to show moral support. Times were desperate. He kept smiling and calling me, 'champ'.

"I'm not going to see him." I mumbled as I got off the number 24 bus; much to the alarm of my fellow passengers. I'd taken this route every day for the past four months to RM Smith's lair. Like a lamb to the slaughter. Was every sacrifice so willing?

He can rot in hell. They all can. It's over.

It'll never be over.

I wandered into Boots. Two for one. Great. Mass consumerism should fill that gaping void.

No, there wasn't a void. It's a chasm. A dark, empty chasm.

No! I was only feeling like this because somehow I kept putting myself on path to destruction.

"Argh!" I stamped my foot. This wasn't my fault. None of this was my fault.

"Hey Jen, you ok?" Janice touched my arm.

"You were talking to yourself." David looked concerned.

"Have I died and gone to hell?" Two for one on this pair was an offer no one wanted. Only, it was actually nice to see them out in the wild.

Of course Janice was here. As the bride of Chucky she'd be bankrupt without the good old two for one. Only, what were they doing here together?

"I'm just having a bit of a mental breakdown. Don't worry about it. I'm on about three a year." The familiar sense of shame came clouding back. The whole office would know why I left.

"Clint told us." Janice lowered her eyes to the ground. "You know that Bank Manager."

"The one who destroyed my life? Yes, I have a vague recollection of him."

I was surprised that Janice and David knew him. Clint had obviously been kept away from the office whilst I was there.

"He saw you at the opera." David frowned as though that location was inconceivable. "You never said you had your own business."

"You never said you like opera." Janice pulled a face – the muscles moved more freely.

"You never asked." I snapped, needlessly defensive.

Janice eyes lit up. "I heard what you called Clint." She smiled wickedly.

There seemed less of a crack to her foundation. It was only Monday I suppose. She'd have been restored to factory settings at the weekend.

"I misheard his name. That's all."

David laughed. "I think you were right with the first hearing."

I thought David would have been more judgemental. It would be fair to think my dalliance with Ron was what kept me on the payroll.

"Did he know who I was when I got the job?" I'd decided my new thing was shooting the elephant in the room. Well, not shooting. That's needlessly aggressive. Just, pointing and shouting, 'look at that elephant'. So everyone could hear; so no one can ignore it.

"Ron?" David clarified to give himself time to think.

I cringed at the name.

"I thought you owned him money. I expected you'd run up a bit of credit card debt."

"Buying magic beans." Janice sneered.

David nudged her playfully before continuingly more solemnly, as though we were at some kind of wake for the tragic death of my career.

"I think he thought you had some Machiavellian scheme to bring the place down from the inside. I told him you weren't that..."

"Clever?"

"No." David looked genuinely appalled. "I told him you weren't that vindictive."

I dared to make eye contact. Sincerity. The same look I'd glimpsed in Carol. David actually liked me. Despite the daily altercations around my time keeping, my 'bloody awful attitude' and 'complete contempt' for the increasingly meaningless tasks, he actually liked me.

"Keep your enemies close then." I smiled, or tried to. My face finally seemed to have forgotten how.

"I'm sure it wasn't like that." Janice stroked my arm. Not her too. Pity would have been easier to deal with than this genuine affection.

"Try not to hate him." David appealed.

"He's enough enemies I suppose. Have they caught the resident artist yet?"

The look passed between them again.

"It's a bit awkward." Janice lowered her voice. "Geoff had this crazy idea about Dave and I."

I was proud of myself. Turns out one of the men was called Geoff.

"He prefers to be called David." I corrected Janice.

Another look passed between the pair and it was confirmed Geoff's idea may not have been so wild.

"Dave!" I beamed. "You're the wanker!"

"It's not funny." David flushed. "Ron's really annoyed."

"You know, Dave." I feigned sincerity. "There are two words that have been invaluable to me throughout all my trials these past six months."

They book looked at me expectantly.

"Oh, well." I smiled. "It's bloody hilarious that you're the wanker." Only, confusing too. "I thought Ron would have loads of people he screwed over lining up to deface his building."

"Ron doesn't screw people over. If all had gone well with your business you would have a very different view of Smiths."

David was being unreasonable again and pointing out the obvious. He might get bumped back to Dave.

"I wouldn't have known any of you." That pained me. "You'll both keep in touch?"

"No choice." David frowned. "We're struggling with your filing system."

"Ah, well, you would." I sounded all knowledgeable. As if there had actually been a system.

"He's lost without you." Janice blurted.

"I can understand that." I deliberately misinterpreted the statement. "I was pretty much your right hand guy, wasn't I Dave?"

"You know what she means."

"There's no chance you could forgive Ron?" Janice ventured.

"None." I'd never forgive either of them. "They don't deserve it."

"Maybe not." Janice conceded. "But you do."

CHAPTER 30

So, from 'definitely not bloody going' to back where it all started.

He looked older as I approached the table. Not at all like the man I thought I knew. He looked anxious too. Like the first time we met. It had been endearing then. Now, I didn't know what to feel. It saddened me that I didn't really feel anything.

He hadn't noticed I'd arrived. I watched him in those unguarded moments; when he didn't have to pretend. The man I used to love. The man I knew, as I dispassionately observed him, that I no longer loved.

It was hard to recall why I'd been so impressed. The future I'd allowed myself to dream of died the day he betrayed me. There was no road back for us now. When his worried little eyes caught mine all I saw was the past.

"Hello, Stephen."

He leapt from his chair. "I didn't think you'd come."

Neither did I.

He tried to kiss me on the cheek. I pulled back awkwardly. There was no social convention for how we should greet each other now.

I sat down opposite him and repressed the urge to make a flippant and demeaning comment like, 'how's the book going?'

I opted for the safer, less contentious, "It's weird being back here."

Everything about this was weird.

The Ram's Head had been our local pub. Well, it had been his local when we'd got together and, somehow, it had become ours. Much like the Bookshop. His dream had merged with mine to produce something neither of us really wanted.

I didn't particularly like The Ram's Head but I could have used it as a bargaining chip in the spoils of war if we had simply separated. Stephen could have got sole custody of this place and, he could have felt like he'd won.

"I haven't been with anyone else." Stephen reached out for my hand. As though his sexual fidelity was the highest stake.

I let him take my hand; just to check.

I felt nothing.

Test over. I pulled my hand away.

"Stephen, what you did." There were just no words.

There had been nights I'd lain awake wondering how he was spending my money and with whom. Those nights had long since passed.

"I know. I'm sorry. And, I know how inadequate sorry is." He put his head in his hands and seemed to look penitent but, there was an edge to his tone. As though I should have been grateful to see him. Relieved that he had come to save the day.

"Your hair's longer than I remember." He'd finally managed a beard of sorts too.

Stephen shifted awkwardly in his chair. He'd been trying to conceal his identity as he hid in plain sight.

"Ah, I see."

He had the decency to look embarrassed under the sparse facial hair.

"Why did you call?" Now I was here it felt again like a bad idea. Like throwing salt in open wounds.

Stephen shrugged. "My lawyer told me not to reach out."

I hadn't even told my lawyer. Another bad decision. Just keep racking them up, Jen.

"I couldn't stay away." Tears filled his eyes.

"You managed fairly successfully for six months."

"I know." Stephen looked as though he was going to cry. His tears had not been uncommon in our relationship. I come to think of them now as a tool he used to cause my distress. His emotional state was quick to change; when he got what he wanted.

"The moment I left I wanted to come back but how could I?"

Easily.

"After what I'd done."

180

I knew Stephen was asking a different question; how could I come back and face no consequence for my actions?

The tears flowed down his face unchecked and unashamed. I reached out instinctively and took his hand. I hadn't even realised I was doing it.

"Here." I handed him a tissue. Well, a napkin from the cutlery bucket on the table. I'm not Mother Theresa.

Ron always had proper handkerchiefs.

No, Ron is a tool. Don't think about him either.

"I've screwed it all up." Stephen wiped the tears away with the back of his hand. "I'll never be able to repay you."

"The insurance will cover it." That was quite a helpful turn of events; it seemed I owned them now.

"That's not what I meant. I can't take away the pain and worry of the past few months. I have to live with what I did."

"Yeah." I sighed. "You will."

And he was crying, again.

"You look amazing." He gasped through the tears. Finding that apparently more distressing. "I was wrong about you not suiting highlights in your hair."

Mum smiled when she'd seen the new hairdo. 'It's great to have the old you back.' The me I'd allowed him to slowly erode. I heard his words fall through time, 'you suit your hair dark,' 'Carol always had it in for me and I don't think she's that fond of you either.' "Those are your friends, of course they would say that. They don't

181

have my best interests at heart.' Subtly, over time, he'd chipped away at me to create what he wanted and, somehow, I'd let him.

The Bookshop sold music because that's what Stephen wanted. I'd stood by as shiftless hipsters took over the place because it made Stephen happy. I moulded into him in the same way I'd despised Janice for on that 'have a date with a serial killer website' she was so fond of. Oh no! I felt the revelation coming this time. *I didn't hate Janice. I hated the part of me I saw in her.*

Stephen looked at me expectantly. He wanted me to make this all ok. He wanted me to expunge yet another of his mistakes from history. That had been my role in our relationship but I couldn't, wouldn't, delete this one.

"It was a shitty, shitty thing that you did but," I ordered a large glass of wine. "I learned a lot of things I'd never have found out if we'd just dodged along."

"That I'm a treacherous cretin." Stephen slumped further in his chair. How could this still be about him?

"I learnt that I'm a hell of a lot stronger than I thought. My world fell apart and I got up. I got a job. I made a financial plan and somehow, despite being an utter cow to anyone who crossed my path, I made new friends. I reconnected with old ones. I fell in love."

"You what?"

I told myself that I didn't believe in love at first sight. I told myself it had been far too early for love but, I told myself to trust my instincts. I was still in love with Ron. I just wasn't going to do anything about it.

"This has been the most challenging six months of my life but," I smiled; relieved to know my muscles had found that movement again. "Genuinely, it hasn't been the worst."

"You fell in love?"

"You ran off with my life savings, Stephen. You've kinda lost the moral high ground." I took a deep breath and tried to remain serene.

"You did a crappy, crappy thing but you didn't break me."

I did that all by myself.

I'd built my life around a man who only had his own interests at heart. 'Never put the keys to your happiness in someone else's pocket' was the latest social media tag from Mum.

"Is that why you're here? To gloat about the new man in your life?" His voice suddenly bitter. I remembered how, slowly, over the course of an argument, he would make everything my fault.

"We had seven years together. You were the first man I ever loved..."

"Stop it. I don't want to hear you say it."

"I don't want there to be animosity between us. If I pass you, or your family on the street one day, I want us all to say hello. I want us to remember more than this passed between us."

"You should hate me. I hate me!"

Whatever I did for Stephen, it would never be enough.

"I did hate you, or I tried to and it damn near killed me." Suddenly I could have given the good Lord Buddha a run for his money. It was as though a light had finally gone on in my head.

"I spent so much time hating you and being bitter I was constantly drained and exhausted. I nearly missed out on all the amazing things this bloody nightmare had to offer. You see Stephen, this wasn't just about you. The ship doesn't sink because it's surrounded by water. It sinks because the water gets inside." I could feel my heart swell at the love Carol had shown in dragging me from that pit of a bed.

"What the hell does that mean?"

"It means that this is over. I forgive you." The words I never thought I would say lifted the weight I'd been carrying around in my stomach for months.

"I don't deserve that." And, for the first time in years, Stephen looked like he meant it.

"Maybe not, but I do." I stood up and grabbed my coat. "I've given a statement to my lawyer that says some nice things about you. It might help at the trial. Truly, no hard feelings."

"Please stay, I want to tell you about Brighton. I always wanted to come back to you."

I kissed him on the cheek. "But I'm not the woman you left."

Stephen saw the transformation of the past few months and credited it to another. "What's he like, this new guy?"

I couldn't think about him. That wound was still raw. Lord Buddha still had the edge.

"This place is all yours now." I smiled, looking around affectionately. We'd had some good times here too.

"I really did miss you." Stephen whispered, as though admitting a terrible secret. "I came back because..." His voice trailed off. He had come back because his mother was sick. He had come back because the money was gone and there was nowhere else to go. Of all the reasons he had come back, I wasn't one of them. We'd come to the end of the line many times before and I'd always let him pull me back in. This time the bond between us was severed. In the story of my life he deserved only a passing mention. I'd wasted enough time here.

I allowed myself to remember happier times.

"I hope your Mum gets better soon. Let everyone know that I'm thinking of them."

Not the fact they knew where you were, what you'd done and were quite happy to be complicit in screwing me over.

This was it. This is what closure felt like. I turned to go.

"Wait," Stephen stood up and reached into his bag. "I want you to have this."

And there it was. As dog eared and beaten up as ever. My signed copy of *The Hitchhikers Guide to the Galaxy*.

CHAPTER 31

"It wasn't about the book." The words had come from everyone else then, finally, me.

"You don't say." Carol offered up mock surprise.

"I might have heard that somewhere before." Mum pretended to look thoughtful.

I was the last one to understand. It wasn't until I held that tattered thing in my hand I finally understood.

Mum poured us both a coffee. I hadn't drunk the last one. Dad's full cup sat on the kitchen table between us. He had been optimistic about joining us until he saw the time bomb I held in my hand.

"If it was about the book," I turned what had been my prized possession over in my hand. "I should feel better now that I have it back. Shouldn't it?"

Mum shrugged as she exchanged another meaningful look with Carol. Mum was dying to tell me something but being a parent meant letting me find out for myself. No matter how painful. Or, how much devastation I left in my wake.

"It was all the other stuff either, was it?" I whispered. I had to be sure. I knew the revelation that was coming was important. I was pretty sure the kitchen had been painted another shades lighter and no one had even mentioned it.

When Stephen walked out he took not only our future but our past; the life we'd had together, the person I thought he was. The idea of who we were, who I was within that, evaporated in a second. The book represented all I had held dear; including him. Much as I had treasured this possession it wasn't the book I'd wanted back. It was that life. I wanted to be the girl I was before any of this; hopeful, optimistic and believing I had the world at my feet. Now the book was a potent reminder there was no way back. Like everything else, including me, it was tarnished by this whole experience.

"Maybe I'll just sell it. Someone else might appreciate it more." I was tempted to just throw it in the bin. I never wanted to see it again.

"Don't you dare!" Mum picked the book up defensively. "Jen, I've never been prouder of you than I have been this past six months."

"I've been to University. I had my own business and, really? It was the bankruptcy court and fraud squad that earned me the greatest daughter of the year mug?"

"It earned you something." Carol retorted.

"You're right." Carol looked as though the words chocked her. She'd had to say that a lot recently. "This past few months has given you more than another six dodging along with that idiot ever would."

Mum tried to hand back the ragged, tired, old book. I didn't take it.

"I was a nicer person before all this."

"You needed to toughen up." Carol from the school of hard knocks declared. "You were too nice."

"Can someone be too nice?" It was a genuine question.

"You were always a bit flighty. You found it hard to settle on things and concentrate in school. That doctor wanted to medicate you to help you focus but..."

"What was that?"

"Ah, it was all in the past." Mum waved her hand dismissively.

"I worried the one thing you managed to maintain your attention on was Stephen."

"Who, no offence," Carol interjected, "always seemed like a complete waste of oxygen on this dying planet you care so much about." She took a large gulp of her scalding hot coffee so she could avoid eye contact.

"I should have seen it coming. Maybe I would have if you'd just medicated me."

"None of us saw this coming." Carol assured. "I didn't think Stephen had the balls."

"You need to let yourself off the hook, love." Mum didn't want to talk about Stephen's balls so close to lunch. "It's over."

"It's hard to think I could resent something I once treasured." Harder still to accept the book could be a reminder of anything other than this time.

"You've had that book since you were twelve years old. It's part of your story. What it means to you, and what happens from here on in, well, that's up to you." Mum held the book out again.

"This isn't about what he took, Jen. You have a new job, a new flat. You don't have to reject Ron just to make a point." Carol asserted.

"We weren't talking about Ron." His name was banned. I made people put money in a jar when they uttered it. I was going to buy a new handbag.

"Isn't that the elephant in the room?" Carol almost shouted. "They fact that we should be talking about Ron? The fact that you're punishing him for the things that Stephen did to you."

"I'm not punishing anyone." I tried to sound confident. I wasn't. "I'm making better choices."

"That's the thing with choices, love," Mum distracted herself in brushing a few stray crumbs from the table. "You can always make a different one."

CHAPTER 32

"Adult learning?" David looked at me with disbelief.

"You need a reference because you want to teach adults to read and write?"

"Yip. Wanna come?" I took a drink of wine. "Sorry. Old habits die hard."

"Why are you apologising? It was funny." David ordered another Gin and Tonic, despite his earlier protests that we shouldn't be meeting in a bar at lunch time on a work day. I couldn't have gone to the office. Ron would be there.

"I'm trying to be nicer you prick." I smiled, "It's a work in progress."

"Fine." He pushed the form into his pocket.

I needed a reference from my most recent employer. I couldn't ask Ron. What would he say? 'Not bad in the sack'. I'd been nervous enough about contacting David. He'd been way more patient with me over the months than I'd deserved.

"And you'll say nice things?" I really wanted this job. This was what I'd wanted to do. The trendy Bookshop had been Stephen's idea.

"I'll lie like a bandit. Anything to keep you out of my office." David grinned.

"I wasn't the easiest person to work with I..."

"Was depressed." He broke in with an understanding nod.

"I was going for 'total bitch' but sure, your explanation's nicer."

David sniffed his glass. "I hope this isn't a double. I don't want to go back to the office stinking of booze."

"You don't want to be the only one not to either. I was actually high most of the time."

"That would explain your filing system."

I was suddenly anxious I should have been putting those documents somewhere other than the shredder. Still, from what I hear twenty five per cent of the server is still 'inoperable' so there could be any manner of data losses.

David looked at me thoughtfully. "It's just business, Jen. What happened to you was really crap but it's also really rare. Ron..."

I held up my hand. I didn't want to hear Ron missed me as much as I missed him. I didn't want to acknowledge, even to myself, that despite life going so well there was something, someone missing. I tried every day not to think about how much I missed Ron. Or all the different ways that I missed him. Like the way he'd catch my eye, smile and silence the inner storm. Or the way his confidence inspired me to be more self-assured. Or the way I missed being held by him, touched by him and that feeling of being completely understood. I tried not to think if I'd missed finding out what could have become of us.

"That man is dead to me."   I mustered more confidence than I'd thought possible.

"Ok," David sighed, "but, the deceased is, sorry, was," he corrected.

I couldn't help but smile.

"He was a good boss. He gave people way more chances than they deserved and he didn't fire you as he should have done for your poor time keeping, shitty attitude and complete disinterest."

"You're not going to say any of that when the Adult Learning Centre call."

David wasn't going to allow me to be flippant. "He misses you. He keeps that blooming Spiderman lunch box on his desk."

"Power Rangers." I corrected. "He can keep it. Belonged to Stephen." That felt like a little triumph.

"It doesn't matter who it belonged to. You gave it to him." David looked compassionate. As though he was trying to elicit a similar feeling in me.

"I gave him my flat and my old business. Does he keep them on his desk too?"

David was a literal thinker. I saw the momentary confusion and watched as he suppressed the urge to tell me neither would fit. He seemed so perplexed by the intrusive verbal image that completely missed the point.

"Ron hangs around the office when Janice and I talk about you."

"Aw, you still talk about me?" I wanted to change the subject.

"All the time. We talk about how professional you were. How much we miss your efficiency and how we definitely haven't spent the past weeks clearing up your cock ups."

A little, ok large, part of me had to admit I should have been sacked a long time ago.

"Why didn't you send me packing?" Ron maybe should have fired me but David could have. Many times.

David shrugged, as though it wasn't a big deal. "You'd clearly had some kind of negative life changing event." Then he laughed. "Besides, you added a bit of colour to the place."

"And Ron wouldn't let you, right?"

David looked at the floor. I'd perfected Ron's trick of continuing to look at the person after the awkward question to tease out the answer.

"I thought he felt he owed you."

"Nope, I owed him. Thousands. He probably kept me there so I didn't default on the payments."

David considered the response. "You sort of cost us more to have there. I mean, correcting the..."

"Training needs?" I offered, helpfully.

David took another drink. "I was going to say cock ups."

I should have protested but there were too many to count. The time I'd meant to e-mail admin and accidently sent an attachment containing everyone's salary to 'all staff'. David had covered that one up with an impromptu fire drill and an instant email recall. Sometimes it was incompetence. Sometimes it was complete disinterest. I couldn't have been the only one hating me at Smiths.

"I bet my name is mud back at the office." I thought of the swarm of nameless faces.

"It's yesterday's news now."

I wanted to ask what had happened today.

"Has the graffiti stopped?"

David held his breath.

"You know, what's-his-face might not be way of the mark with his suspicions about you and Janice."

"She's never off those bloody dating apps!" Said the man who had been following her around *Boots* as thought shopping for make-up is a normal thing to do with a colleague.

"Good, that means she's still available. You know, Dave." I felt myself get all serious. "It's not too late but one day it might be."

"You think she'll find someone?" The anxiety clear in his tone.

"Or be murdered." That felt the more likely outcome.

There was a silence between us. One I knew that I shouldn't fill. David needed time to consider what he would do.

"Maybe." Was all he would commit to.

"Well, at least my replacement can't be any worse."

David shifted awkwardly again in his chair.

Of course I hadn't been replaced. I did sod all.

"I suppose they are pretty big shoes to fill. I can only imagine the robust recruitment process you have in place."

David smiled, relieved. "Don't change too much. Will you?"

CHAPTER 33

Mum buzzed around my new flat.

"This is amazing, love!" She cleaned excitedly as she went. The place had been professionally cleaned but that was Mum; doubly cautious. I should be more like Mum.

"It's going to be strange just me and your father at home. Are you sure you'll be alright living here alone?"

"You're not moving in."

Mum beamed in the way that parents who adore their children do when they see the offspring finally happy. And I was happy. Mostly.

I'd decided that Ron was like an appendix. I'd Googled it last night. It's not an organ. Just a piece of tissue. Some kind of evolutionary leftover (how apt for a man of his advanced years) and, you can live without it.

"It is genuinely lovely." Mum looked around for the millionth time just to check the place hadn't changed.

"So lucky not to have anyone above you like the last place."

I'd forgotten how much I complained about my old neighbours. It was like the cast of River Dance rehearsing in clogs above us and, through the wall to the left, what I can only imagine were porn stars. The sex noises were unbelievable! Once, when Dad was visiting. He just about coped. Dad turned the TV up to that supersonic volume only parents were able to find. It didn't help.

Maybe I did idealise that time of my life. I was living more in the present. I'd call in mindfulness but then I'd want to punch myself in the face. I was rebuilding my life. Chumba wumbaing like a legend. I should have been proud of myself and, I was. At least, that's the face that I showed the rest of the world. Happy, care free, Jen; the one who was still broken inside. The pain of this break up was different from that of Stephen's. This one physically hurt.

Mum stopped frantically cleaning. "I wasn't sure if I should say but, he came around the other night. The man from your work."

"David?" I began examining the empty kitchen. Not long before this would be a war zone of half-eaten cereal packs, discarded tea bags and mouldy old cheese. Then, I remembered, that too had been Stephen. I had just given up trying to clean up after him.

I'd seen more of Janice and David recently. We'd often go for drinks and talk about the good old days. Well, all of the mistakes I made and how they'd fixed them. Turns out I was right about Janice. I didn't really hate her. Well, I don't hate her as much anyway.

"Ron."

I looked cautiously at Mum.

"I have to admit I was a bit..."

"Shocked?" I hadn't told Mum much about Ron. Except that I hated him; well, I was trying too.

"Surprised." She acknowledged but there was no judgement in her tone. "He was a bit older than..."

"Methuselah?"

"Than I expected." She continued.

Mum motioned for me to sit down next to her on the sofa. She rarely asked me to be focused on one thing at once; probably because she didn't let me have the pills when I was a kid. I wondered what version of Jen I could have become with them. Mum's request for my undivided attention indicated this was important.

"I get it." She smiled. "He seemed genuinely lovely. Warm, open..."

"You know he foreclosed on the loan. He caused all this!"

Mum looked around my wonderful new flat. "Then he did good. And, he didn't cause this, love. This didn't have one cause. This was a whole series of causes that ended here and," she looked around. "This is just another beginning."

Mum's free styling with the inspirational quotes now.

"He didn't actually meet you until two months after the event."

I hated it when parents were all reasonable in pointing things out.

"Did he tell you that? Did he tell you he was a grandfather? He could be older than you."

"He's not. It wouldn't much matter if he was." Mum continued calmly.

"He said he was sorry and that he loved you. He wanted to be sure you were alright. That you were happy. I wasn't supposed to tell you. He made me swear but, I wanted you to know. I wanted you to make an informed choice."

"About what?" There was no choice to be made.

"It's not too late."

"For what?" I challenged. There was no way back from this.

"It's not too late for us to live happily ever after?" I mocked. "If we hooked up you could be someone's great grandmother. Think about that."

Mum wouldn't be railroaded. "This isn't about me, love." She began picking at the hem of her t-shirt. She wasn't going to allow my attention to move on.

"All I'm saying is it's not too late but, one day, it will be."

"Because he'll be dead. Because he's ancient. Time isn't exactly on his side."

Mum looked thoughtful. "So why would you waste any more of it?"

Of course I wanted to be with Ron. I had to wake up each day and remind myself it was a terrible idea. The

200

pain would pass and I would be a better person for having endured it. Going back to Ron would be an easy answer. A quick fix. Stephen had taught me the danger of those.

"I can't keep bouncing from one disaster to the next." Maybe Mum was wrong. Maybe all of these events did have the one cause; maybe it was me.

"If you don't want to be with him then, don't. But he seems to really get you."

One day I'd asked Ron what he'd do if he was chased by a lion. For a moment he looked as though he was about to have me committed. Then he'd asked, quite thoughtfully, 'how big is the lion and where am I?' I appreciated the follow up. It showed me he was talking the question seriously. Stephen would have told me to grow up. Then trot off to 'work' (spend hours in the library 'researching' zombies) with his Power Rangers packed lunch box. Being with Stephen had been exhausting. He was constantly trying to make me something I wasn't; someone I didn't want to be. I let him because being in a couple helped me 'fit'. Only, it was into a world I didn't want to belong. In a way, I was glad when Stephen left. I was glad it had finally ended.

Stephen and Ron were not the only two men on the planet. But I'd never really met anyone who understood how my mind worked like Ron did. My brain would race from one thing to another with no logical thought pattern. I've never felt as focused, or as calm, as I did with him.

"Mum," I ventured. "Remember when you said those doctors wanted to medicate me."

She laughed. "You were just quirky, love."

Yeah, apparently clinically so.

CHAPTER 34

That's the thing about Armageddon. Sometimes the world has to end for it to begin again. Ron said something similar about a phoenix rising from its own ashes. No, he didn't. He said, 'I'm a treacherous Hell Hound. Stay away.' Or he should have. Only, I wouldn't have listened. I didn't want to play safe. The greatest philosopher of our time, Taylor Swift, put it most succinctly when she said: 'don't you know I love the players and, you love the game.' Only, Ron wasn't a player. He had a slightly arthritic knee.

Ron didn't know me. He couldn't have. I didn't know myself. Ron could only have seen what Stephen did; a malleable form to be shaped into what he wanted. I thought about it and realised I couldn't choose Ron. I couldn't make my life about another man. I built my world around Stephen, or let him create my world with him at the centre. Whatever happened, when Stephen left, I didn't belong.

Mum tagged me in another inspirational quote on social media this morning. 'You might not be where you want to be but, you're not where you were.' Is it mega callous to consider blocking your own mother? I'd do it too, if I wasn't genuinely concerned she'd get sucked in to some kind of online moon worshipping cult. Honestly, that woman has given away enough personal information on social media for strangers to open loan applications. Twice.

Anyway, Ron had stopped calling. There was no decision to be made. The decision had made itself. Time was not only the greatest healer and teacher, (although it's a bit harsh killing all one's students), Time it seems, is also the last word in decision making.

"Another coffee?" The waitress approached the table of the swanky new coffee shop that had only this week replaced Hype.

"I'm ok, thanks." I was more than ok. I'd mastered sitting and eating alone. I'd gone off the deep end too. This place held so many memories and I faced up to each and every one of them. No laptop, no mobile phone, no book; no pretence. Just me, myself and I. Sitting here, drinking coffee, like an utter psychopath. I didn't need to pretend to the outside world I was taking 'time out for me'. I no longer had to justify and explain myself to a disinterested planet. Today I was doing something far more important. Today, I was forgiving one of the most important people of all. I was forgiving myself.

I'd spent months blaming everyone else but, in the cold light of day, I should have read the small print on a massive loan application. I would have known who foreclosed on the loan, and why. The shop was supposed to have been a joint venture but it was all in my name. Stephen had been too risk adverse. Too worried that if things were to go wrong he'd ruin his future. He was quite happy to ruin mine. I'd been anxious too but I'd invested too much in the relationship; the dream. I should have been honest. I should have told Stephen I resented him. Before he left I'd actually come to quite dislike him. Distance had grown between us. Habit was all that kept up together. Habit or all the comfort my hard work continued to provide. He'd taken advantage of me for months.

I lost myself in Stephen. I stayed and never thought to ask him to leave because he had become the axis of my existence and, I didn't even like him. So, I'd no chance of liking me. The bitterness and the sarcasm set in long before he left. Love shouldn't do that. Love shouldn't make you feel like you're in someone else's debt. I owed Ron thousands and never once felt like anything but his equal. On the lowest rung of his organisational ladder he treated me with as much respect and dignity as he did the board of directors. I mean, honestly, I quite fancy seeing my old job description again. Apparently I should not have been so focussed on shredding.

I'd tried to protest to Mum that choosing Ron wasn't a valid option. As though convincing her would be some kind of victory. Some kind of validation.

'This isn't about what I want. It's about what I need.'

She'd just smiled serenely, 'you know love, sometimes it's the same thing.'

"Are you ok?" The waitress looked anxiously at my empty cup and the growing number of people waiting at the door.

I picked up my wallet distractedly to pay. "I was just thinking about my appendix and how I don't really need it."

She started counting the change I'd laid out on the table. "They've changed their mind about that." She smiled realising there was indeed a generous tip.

No, the waitress was wrong. It was an evolutionary left over. "It's just a tiny bit of useless skin that at any minute could flare up and kill us."

"I think it has something to do with digestion." She puzzled. "Look at all the millions of people on the planet with an appendix. How many of them have actually been killed by it?"

My research hadn't gone that far.

"Sure, it's something you can live without," she pocketed the money, "but why would you?"

"Actually, do you mind if I have five minute to make a quick call?"

The waitress shrugged and moved on. She had her tip and we all knew in a month's time this place would be something else anyway.

I picked up my mobile phone, withholding my number because I hadn't quite got full value in the cray cray stakes. No, it was because I only wanted to leave a message. A message where I could say what I wanted, without questions or interruptions. I pleaded with a deity that I had long since spurned that Ron was busy or screening his calls. After six months of Hell, God realised She owed me.

"Hey, it's..." He'd know. "I... I don't hate you. I shouldn't have said that. But, being in a relationship means being brutally honest. Telling someone what they don't want to hear. What you don't want them to know. I mean, not like they have huge thighs or..." *Stay focussed Jen*. "It hurt. It hurt because..."

The phone clicked and I ended the call.

"I love you." I whispered into the dead air.

CHAPTER 35

I had to tell Ron to his face. Telling someone you loved them wasn't a voicemail or text situation. Unless you had told them a hundred times before and even then you had to be careful. When Dad text Mum to tell her Aunty Val had died she should not have replied, 'lol'. In Mum's defence she had thought it meant, 'lots of love' rather than 'laughed out loud'. I'd had to have another conversation with my parents about the kind of information that can be shared by text and on social media. Val's children were less than impressed that Aunty Suzie found the death of their mother funny. They still don't sent a Christmas card.

I walked with purpose down the street. I impressed myself with the determination and focus. Uncharacteristically, I didn't stop to look at anything shiny. I didn't even notice those patent red shoes. Ok, I did, but I'd go back later. I mean I had purpose, I wasn't dead.

Hastily I redialled. "Look, I'm just going to pop in and see you. Five minutes. There's something I need to say and then, I just need a bit more time."

Time to sort my head out. Time to build a world that could merge with his to become ours. I needed time to come to terms with all that happened in the past six months. Time to separate my mistakes from Stephen's and Stephen's from Ron's. Right now I was blaming everyone for everything and the only chance Ron and I had at a future was for me to move on from the past. If Ron loved me he'd wait. If he didn't, my heart sank at the thought. Well, if he didn't then, I'd know. Knowing was better than this. Here and now Ron and I were nothing. Nothing but two people who'd hurt each other. I didn't want that to be the final word for us.

Now the whole debacle was all finally over I had to face some difficult truths. I hadn't missed Stephen. I missed the place in the world he'd given me; but it wasn't my place, it wasn't my world. Missing having someone to lie next to at night is not the same is missing that actual living breathing person. I needed to know I could do life on my own and it seemed that I can. New flat, new job, new social life and still, I missed Ron. I wanted him in my life. That was the difference. Ron was my appendix. I could live without him; I just didn't want to.

In what had felt like a world of all consuming darkness Ron had shone a light and yes, he wasn't the only one but somehow, his was the only light that got through. Ron knew me better than I knew myself. He saw through the bravado designed to push people away and we connected. Being with Ron was exciting and comforting in equal measures. Maybe it would never work out. Maybe we were worlds and not just generations apart but we'd never know unless we tried. Really and properly tried. Rejecting Ron wasn't the smart thing to do. It wasn't brave. It was the opposite of both those things.

I think.

I turned the corner onto the main street. Smiths loomed before me. My pace dropped. I hadn't thought about walking in. I hadn't even considered when I did Ron might not be there. As though answering another little prayer he drew up in his car and bounded out. Ron looked far more chipper than I'd imagined. I put aside the churlish thought that he should be bereft and the fleeting question of why he'd stopped calling. I stepped forward, about to call out when I realised. Someone was with him.

CHAPTER 36

Don't jump to conclusions Jen.

My heart raced. I felt sick.

Ron was with someone else.

I watched as he smiled and threw his arms affectionately around the most beautiful woman I'd ever seen. He kissed her cheek, and stroked the hair from her face. Long, beautiful blonde hair paired with olive, sun kissed skin. I never tanned like that. The most I could hope for was all my freckles would join up to give a slight colour change. Usually the best I could muster was a fairly good likeness to a lobster.

Ok. I took a deep breath. Well, I'd come to ask Ron to wait and now, I had my answer. Maybe in opening his heart I'd allowed another to walk through. Maybe he'd given her the tortured, 'I've never loved anyone since my wife' routine. Or she too was just paying off a debt. We all have our patterns; maybe this was his. Our time together had been a series of lies.

Jen, stop. It doesn't matter what he's saying, what he's doing. You have your answer.

Ron caught my eye. He pulled away from the goddess.

"Jen!" He waved his hand as though I hadn't seen him. As though I hadn't been watching it all unfold.

I'd edged closer than I'd realised. As if to punish myself further. I had to check how beautiful she really was to reinforce my own inadequacy. I wanted to say something profound. Something to show how grown-up, sophisticated and beyond this sordid affair I really was.

She turned to catch a glimpse of me; even more breathtaking from the front.

I opened my mouth to speak. Nothing.

"Jen." Ron stepped forward looking more concerned. As though he realised what I must have seen. As though my opinion of him could have got any lower.

Oh no! The voicemails. He'd have heard those erratic voicemails. They would have listened them together in the car and laughed. The humiliation.

"I... I..." I spun around and ran. Like the proper grown-up I had become.

CHAPTER 37

"This is pretty impressive." Carol looked around the new Community Centre.

"Jimmy, go play with that outside." The resident eight year old hoodlum kept bouncing his football against the wall.

"Sorry." I smiled as Carol wiped the muddy ball print from her pristine white trousers. "There's a washing machine at the back if you want."

"It's ok. They're last seasons." They were also silk and Carol wouldn't be putting them near the industrial machines we had available.

Three months had passed since I walked into the Job Centre and asked Neil for help. It was a fortnight since I had seen Ron with his new love interest and, I was managing to keep afloat. I'd decided now that I'd moved on. I'd not only deleted Ron's number I had changed mine. I refused to listen when my parents told me he'd called or that he turned up again at the house. Mum had told him I was fine. And I was. Well, I would be. Plus, given how impressed I'd been with Ron's new girlfriend maybe I could be gay after all. That opens up a whole new dating market.

Carol was right. My new work place was impressive. "No one is going to be scrawling wanker over this door."

"Wouldn't bet on it." Carol gave me a sly smile and moved towards my parents in the crowd.

"Here." Janice thrust a bunch of flowers in my face. "Well done and all that."

I hadn't recognised her at first. "You look different."

"I had a makeover."

More like a make down. Half of the foundation, at least, was gone.

"You look amazing." It felt unbelievable Janice would have concealed all that beauty under, well, concealer.

"I wore my make up like you wore your sarcasm. It was my mask to the world. When you took yours off, I thought, what the hell."

I beamed triumphantly. "The mentee has become the mentor."

Sure I liked Janice now but it was still fun to wind her up.

"Please don't tell anyone I was your mentor." Janice looked genuinely anxious.

David caught her eye and smiled. It was as though all the tension flew from her body. I understood now why they were in Boots together, why he'd always enjoyed my harsh criticism of her online dating and perhaps why he'd sent me out of the office on so many errands.

"I will tell the world you were my mentor." I smiled mischievously.

"What are you supposed to be doing anyway?" Janice refused to be drawn into conflict.

Janice had sent me a picture earlier about a fish being asked to climb a tree and thinking it was stupid. Janice seemed to have understood my time at Smiths better than I did; just a fish out of water. This was my time to show my strengths and my skills. I just hoped that I had them.

"My job is to support people to develop their communication skills. We're planning on doing job applications, interview preparation, letters to the bank, that kind of thing." Neil and I would be working closely together from now on. Irony layered upon irony.

"Glad to see that you know your job description this time." Janice grinned.

"Well, just remember to keep your coffee away from the IT equipment." She accused. We'd never actually admitted out loud it was me.

"I hope you're managing to cope without me."

"Not all of us." Janice looked at me meaningfully. The same look she used back in the days before the appendix situation. When she wanted to communicate something significant. For old times' sake I ignored her.

"Is it just Dave and I from the office?" Her eyes scanned the faces of the other launch party attendees.

"I don't know anyone else." I wasn't going to take the bait. "There isn't anyone else I would have wanted here." I still couldn't make that sound convincing.

"He misses you." Janice pretended to arrange the flowers in a vase.

Ron, the one thing we never talked about.

"I was a bit surprised when I heard you two were." Janice raised her eyebrow. It was her eyebrow too; the high def/magic marker/footballers wife look was gone.

"It was a one-time thing." We'd had one actual night together, but we'd been connected far longer. *No, that was the past*. This place and the people here are my future.

"Ron doesn't strike me as a one-time-thing kinda guy. I should know." Janice got her retort in first. "I had enough of them."

"How many? I was running a book."

"Was it a book about zombies?" She mocked.

I realised quite quickly into our post work socials not only did I not hate Janice, I actually quite liked her.

"Ron talked the Police into leniency with Stephen. Said the poor guy had suffered enough. Which he hadn't."

That's how I knew Janice and I were friends. She hated Stephen with a venom not even I could muster now. I'd spent so much time being angry and alienating people I was truly shocked that when the sadness finally broke, they saw it and reached out. I only recently understood too they'd seen the sadness before I did; hidden in all the anger.

"I don't think he gives a shit about Stephen. He just wanted all of this to be over for you."

David approached with a glass of fizzy no alcohol wine.

"Is Ron here?" He rushed the words. "I think he wanted to come but, he wasn't sure he'd be welcome."

"I expect he was busy." I heard the bitterness in my voice as I thought of Ron's gorgeous new blonde.

I hadn't been aware that Janice and David had formed the Ron appreciation society. Perhaps they should have natty little badges warning others of their new affiliations.

"I said he should pop in. Give you the book and see what happens. You only live once, right?" David looked at Janice who stared thunderously back. "What?" He placed his hand casually around her waist.

"What book?" I asked.

David looked more cautiously at Janice. "That signed edition of the *Hitchhikers Guide to the Galaxy*. It took him bloody weeks to track it down."

"How did you know about the book?"

"The whole world knew about that book." Janice groaned. "He had us all searching the internet for it."

The book was a well-rehearsed part of the 'I've lost everything' tirade but Janice and David had been spared it.

217

"The urgency he tracked it down with and then, it just sat and gathered dust on his desk for weeks." David suddenly realised why Janice had been giving him murderous looks and the secret signal to 'shut up'. Hang on, had that signal originally been developed for me?

"Stephen gave me the book back." I assured them. Perhaps Dave and Janice would find the comfort in that gesture that I hadn't.

"No, he did." David protested. "Stephen came into the office on day to apologise. Weedy Fucker." David spat the same venom as Janice.

"It was clearly a tactic to try and worm his way around Ron." David broke off as he saw I genuinely wasn't interested in Stephen. Not anymore.

"Ron had tracked down the book. He gave it to Stephen to give back to you."

"Ron got the book back? I thought Stephen had kept it."

Janice shook her head. "He sold it to an antique book dealer, who sold it to a collector." Janice rolled her eyes this time at David. She gave him the secret signal to shut up.

Anxiety scorched David's face. "Please don't tell him I told you." The anxiety was soon replaced with confusion. "Why go to all that hassle and not take the credit?"

"It wasn't about credit." Janice had suddenly become all sage about relationships. "It was about making Jen happy. Just like when he told the Police to go easy on Stephen."

"I won't tell Ron. I won't see him." I tried again to process what David had said. It was Ron and not Stephen who returned the book.

"I owe you one."

David had given me a 'glowing' reference for this job. I thought it was sweet until I wondered if they were being literal. I'd spilt some hazardous chemical over the paper supply in the office. The whole floor had to be evacuated.

"I'll try not to burn the place down." I tried to shift conversation back to a lighter place but Janice and David would not be deterred.

"It wasn't cheap to get that book back." Janice frowned at David. "Well, it wasn't!"

CHAPTER 38

Carol took my arm and led me from the crowd. "So, Ron got the book back." Our conversation about what the book could mean to me now had new significance.

"Has no one ever told you it's wrong to listen in to other people's conversations?"

"The only conversations worth listening to are the ones people don't know are being monitored." Carol's thoughts seemed to drift elsewhere.

"Are you ok?"

"Could you forgive him?" She turned her attention back to me.

"Is this some kind of test? I thought we all had to save ourselves. Viva la revolution and all of that."

I could try being a lesbian again. Carol had once joked she'd turned gay after a disastrous relationship with a man. She'd started off hating one guy and that hatred extended to the entire male population. It was supposed to make people laugh but, being surrounded by elderly relatives at Gran's funeral was possibly neither the time nor the place. In Carol's defence someone had just asked her an ignorant questions like, 'Which one of you is the man?'

Carol didn't look as though she was trying to trick me. "You have saved yourself."

"I've what?" I teased.

"I'm not saying it. It's ridiculous."

"It's my special day." I pouted.

"You chumba wumbad." She growled. The words sounded as though they might choke her.

"Like a legend." I punched the air.

Carol had sounded ridiculous and that was good for her once in a while. Carol took herself and life way too seriously.

As though to emphasise my point Carol became all sombre. "You worked hard. You failed. You worked harder and, you failed again."

"Is this going somewhere?"

"You have a purpose, " Carol looked around the Centre. "This is all great but I see the sadness, Jen. You're so sad when you think no one's looking. It breaks my heart."

"I'll get over it." *I wouldn't*. Only, I thought that about Stephen.

"Why would you want get over it? You love him."

"It's complicated."

"It's always complicated." She sighed. "Ron's a man of his word. He foreclosed on the loan just like it said in the terms and conditions. He didn't do it to hurt you. He didn't even know you. Yes, he could have told you but then you'd never have got to know him. You'd never have fallen in love."

"I'd have had a choice." Maybe in time I'd learn to be philosophical about it. Ron wasn't 'the one'. Or, at least, he was only 'the one' who showed it was possible to love again. He'd opened up my life for someone else.

I didn't want someone else.

"You have the choice now."

It was probably just unrequited love. Had we had more time the relationship would have fizzled out. Besides, it wasn't just the loan anymore. It wasn't just the age difference. There was the blonde.

"It is too late." I had to hear the words out loud. I tried to tell myself Ron would shift from an older man to an old one fairly soon. I tried to tell myself I'd had a lucky escape.

"You were different with him. Happier. Nicer." Carol smiled, wickedly. "Look maybe it won't last, and maybe you'll get your heart broken all over again but, isn't it worth the risk?"

"I need to protect myself." I looked around the world I had built. People depended on me. I was going to make a difference. I couldn't let them down. I couldn't let me down.

"I don't think I could have another heartbreak." I thought of the days I had to drag myself out of bed. I thought of how devastated I had been when Stephen left. It would be unbearable with Ron.

"I just have to be brave about all of this."

"You're not being brave, Jen. You're being stupid. Life doesn't often give you the chance to be with someone you love. If it does, the smart thing to do is to take it."

"I was horrible." The things I said. The way I had looked at him. His face as he watched me leave.

"I think there might be someone else."

Carol shook her head. "He wouldn't have moved on that quickly. It sounds like he put a lot of effort into finding that book."

He made others put the effort in too. Mr. Business seemed to have all but shut down the department in search of it.

"Ron knew how much that book meant to you, what it represented. He moved heaven and hell to get it back to you and then, took no credit for it. That's a pretty selfless thing to do. Putting aside the fact he gave you a job when no one else would. He kept you on too, even though you were a bloody liability." Carol looked hastily around the crowd, raising her voice slightly. "Not now though, she's great now."

"Can't we talk about something else? Anything else? For example, our mothers both had early menopauses. How are your monthlies? Don't spare any details." Even that conversation would be less awkward than this.

I hated the growing realisation that Carol could be right. Again. Maybe I was being the opposite of brave. Maybe I was being, I don't know, cowardly, cowardly custard.

Carol sighed, "Fine, I've said my piece. We can move on."

"But?" I heard the conjunction in her silence.

Why can't I say things like that out loud?

"Ron was terrified of losing you. That's why he didn't tell you. I'm not excusing any of it Jen but hasn't he proven how much he loves you? In the short time you have known Ron he's done more to help you grow than Stephen ever did. So, I can't help but wonder, if you could give all that love to the wrong man imagine what you could do with the right one?"

"Have you signed up to Mum's motivational quotes?" I tried to be flippant. I tried not to see the truth of what Carol had said.

"Maybe." She paused. "You forgave Stephen."

"But I'm not going to ask him to look after large sums of money for me. I'm not going to let him trample all over me again. I've learned."

Carol's face flashed a deep sadness. "It would be a real shame Jen, if that was all that you'd learned."

CHAPTER 39

The launch of the new Centre had been a massive success. Hundreds of people had come to see what we would be offering and several of the classes were already full.

"In one day you've earned your keep." Neil quipped as he left. He looked much better these days. The new tablets were working well. He'd even been giving Janice the eye. Maybe the tablets were working too well.

I'd asked the others to go on ahead to the pub whilst I locked up. Changed days. The old Jen, the one of Smiths, would have given the keys to someone else. However, this wasn't purely professional. I needed a few moments alone. It was hard being the focus of all this positive attention. Having to pretend life was brilliant. Well, not pretend exactly. Life was brilliant. I'd achieved what I'd set out to do a long time ago and, I was happy. Happy enough. Carol was right. Everyone was right. I still missed him.

I head the door creak behind me. Neil said he'd fix it and then had become embroiled in chatting up the new receptionist Karl. Neil was really living life out loud these days.

"Sorry, we're closed." I should have locked up. Rookie mistake to think everyone could read the sign. "We open again at..."

"Big hairy spiders." His voice took me by surprise.

I swung around.

Ron.

"Hate them. I actually scream. Not a manly scream either. You'd lose all respect for me if you heard it. It's a big girly scream until they scuttle off back to Hell and don't tell me they're more afraid of me. That's not possible."

"What's happening?"

"And my knee hurts." He continued. "Most mornings it's the first thing I feel. Physical pain. I hobble around the flat like an old man. I used to think that was the worst part of the day. It's not. The worst part of the day is waking up and knowing I have to face another one without you. Knowing you hate me."

"I don't hate you." I didn't hate anyone now.

Ron held eye contact. "I got your messages."

Great. I felt my cheeks flush.

"Love means telling someone what they don't want to hear. What you don't want them to know." He paused for breath. "It's not just the spiders, the arthritis and the missing you. I'm not that fond of clowns either."

226

"I said relationships, not love." I hadn't told him that yet. I'd gone to tell him. Then, I'd seen her.

"And, of course you hate clowns." That had to be universal.

I told myself in the small hours of the night that I still had the upper hand. Ron had said that he loved me and I had never said it back. I told myself that was a position of strength and not vulnerability.

"The biggest fear. More than the spiders. Is you might not want to be with me." Ron took a deep breath. "Fine, I'd have to live with that but, you shouldn't be with Stephen either." Then, he turned to go.

"For the record," he paused. "You've gorgeous thighs."

Shit. Had I said that bit out loud? I was suddenly less confident about what I had actually said in the deranged voice mail.

"Porcelain dolls." I didn't want him to leave.

"The people who collect those demonic things have human heads in the attic and bodies bricked up in the walls. Those dolls hold the soul of the tortured dead."

I feared porcelain dolls but, I feared losing Ron more.

He appeared relieved to have a reason to stay. "The sign outside said everyone was welcome."

"We're taking that down. That's how the vampires got in."

Now I understood why the doctors suggested medication. My mind raced. Perhaps Ron had been out

227

with the blonde and realised she'd never be me. But, hell I'd see her. That could only be a good thing.

"I wasn't sure the welcome sign included me. I've been waiting outside for ages. That sounds really creepy but, you weren't taking my calls and I wanted all of this to be your moment." Ron, always so assured, stood awkwardly in the doorway.

"I thought you were coming to see me a few weeks ago then, you seemed spooked and ran off."

"I was." I couldn't explain why I hadn't taken the calls. I felt so many things.

"I was glad to know you had called. Glad to know you were still thinking of me." Still trying to make things right.

Ron looked well. As handsome, perhaps more so, than ever. Damn. Why couldn't he have aged dreadfully? Is it so much to ask that he could have lost his hair, half his teeth, gained a beer belly and twenty pounds. That would be easier. Only, he'd still have those eyes. I'd still love him. I'd still love the sensation when we were together; the peace and the silence.

"Why did you stop calling?"

"I thought it was verging on harassment. Well," Ron blushed. "My lawyer did. He was in the office one day when I'd left the third message with your Mum. He told me you obviously didn't want to speak to me."

I wanted nothing more than to speak to him.

"You're looking good." The words caught my throat. I lost faith in my ability to speak. It felt like I was accusing him of something else.

"I feel like shit." He was trying to remain collected and in control but his voice was cracking and betraying him.

"I miss you. I wish I had told you all of this as soon as I met you."

I wondered what words he would have used. How much I could have hated him from the start?

Stay strong Jen. You don't miss him. It was a one, two, three time thing. All of it a fluke. All of it catching you when you were vulnerable. You're not vulnerable now.

"I'm sure your new girlfriend is..." No, Jen that was bitterness. Think of Lord Buddha. "She seems lovely. You looked happy."

Ron had a right to be happy, even if it wasn't with me. Like that stray cat I'd taken in, fed and had spayed. Eventually I'd had to concede that it wanted to live in squalor with the cat hoarding lady three doors down. Sometimes when you love something, (or tolerate it a bit because you think it makes you a better person) you have to let it go.

Ron did an amazing impression of looking confused. He was a ruthless business man. This was a ploy he would use every day. Except, of course, Ron wasn't ruthless. Everyone had been right about that too.

"The gorgeous blonde, with the amazing figure and skin to die for. The one you had your hands all..."

"I'm going to stop you there." Ron broke in urgently. "The woman whose photograph is all over my flat?"

I shrugged. "I was only there once and I wasn't really taking in the decor."

No Jen, no. Don't think of that night.

Ron flushed at the same memory. The atmosphere charged between us.

"She's my daughter."

The images of the silver framed photographs floated into my mind.

"Is that why you suddenly ran
off?"

"No." I pretended to be interested in the door hinge. "I just forgot I was running in a marathon and going for my personal best."

Ron looked as though he wanted to edge forward but an invisible line had been drawn between us.

"Even I fancied her." That was just weird.

Silence.

"I should have told you about the loan. I should have at least asked if you knew. I tried but, I'd been in a trance for years and from the moment I met you, I felt alive. I want to thank you for that." Ron sounded sincere but, they always do.

"You were right to say everything that you did. In fact, I'd say you were pretty reserved. I just came to tell you, again, that I'm sorry. I respect your choice. Stephen is, well Stephen's beneath you but, if that's your judgement then I trust it."

I didn't trust my judgement. "Stephen?"

"Your Mum said he wanted to get back together. She said you went to meet him that day in town."

"I'd forgotten you and Mum were besties now." Probably even friends on social media. I'd know for sure if Ron drops a few inspirational quotes into the conversation.

"Is that why you stopped calling?"

"That and at the lawyer's insistence. I didn't want to harass you. I just wanted the chance to explain." Ron looked wounded. "You gave Stephen another chance."

"Yes, I went to meet Stephen and yes he did want to get back together but his Mum had the aneurism, not me. I haven't taken leave of my senses. " At least, that's my story and I'm sticking to it. Just don't ask my parents. Or, that doctor I apparently saw as a child.

"I went to see Stephen because Janice was right. Maybe Stephen didn't deserve closure from all of this but, I did."

Ron looked relieved. "We seem to have had quite a bit of confusion lately. So, I want to be clear. I love you, Jen. I have always loved you. I only ever wanted you to be happy. I'd hate to think I'd caused you any lasting pain. If you never want to see me again, and I'm beginning to get that message, then I'll go but, I need to hear it from you." The unuttered implication; when I was calm. I'd been angry for weeks.

"Thank you for the book." The invisible line held steadfast between us.

Ron looked guilty. "Stephen came to the office to apologise and ensure I knew you had nothing to do with the missing money. He didn't know about us. I mentioned you'd told a few people at work about the book...Anyway," he fumbled for words. "I thought you wouldn't have accepted it from me and it was probably more meaningful anyway if he gave it back. I'm sorry if you didn't think that was honest. I just wanted you to have it. Even though, you know, it was never really about the book."

I stepped forward, lowering my voice, closing the distance between us.

"It's always been about the book."

He smiled.

A selfless act. Carol was right, well, not completely right. There's no such thing as totally selfless act because the very act always, always get the girl. The most there could be, the most he could offer, was an act of redemption and he'd completed that weeks ago a hundred times over.

"It wouldn't work out with Stephen." I tried to sound casual. "The truth is I've fallen in love with someone else. Someone who asked me pointed questions and cajoled me into being a better person. Someone who helped me achieve all of this."

"I see." He nodded, resigned. "Thank you for being straight with me. You're young. No doubt you'll fall in love several more times. Neil's a nice guy, if somewhat highly strung."

I rolled my eyes in mock frustration. "And if this is going to work you're going to have to get over the age difference."

"I hope... What?" Ron appeared to have just processed what I said.

"I've known I loved this man since the moment he held my hand at the opera."

"Oh," Ron smiled, stepping closer again. "I see."

Gillian Lee Gibson is a self-published author. *My Own Little Personal Armageddon* is her debut novel. The sequel, *A Bump in the Road*, is available now.

Gillian has a growing collection of darker tales. Her psychological thriller, *Shore Gulls*, is complete and awaiting publication. Gillian is completing her first crime novel, *Dark Angel.*

Gillian has a background in Religious, Moral and Philosophical Studies and currently works as a Psychologist. Gillian draws from this experience and brings a deep understanding of human behaviour and questions of morality to her work.

Please visit Gillian's author's page to keep updated on her recent work.

amazon.com/author/gillian_lee_gibson

Printed in Dunstable, United Kingdom